THE
WORKING
LONGDOG

THE WORKING LONGDOG

FRANK SHEARDOWN

SWAN·HILL
PRESS

First published in the UK in 1989 by Dickson Price Publishers Ltd
This edition published 1999 by Swan Hill Press, an imprint of Airlife Publishing Ltd

British Library Cataloguing-in-Publication Data
A catalogue record for this book
is available from the British Library

ISBN 1 84037 060 2

Printed in England by St Edmundsbury Press Ltd, Bury St Edmunds, Suffolk

Swan Hill Press

an imprint of Airlife Publishing Ltd
101 Longden Road, Shrewsbury, SY3 9EB England.

Contents

Introduction

One's severest critics always seem to lurk near to home and, one day last year just after I had an article on deerhound hybrids published in one of our better known sporting weeklies, I inquired of my friend Joe, as I sank a self-congratulatory pint in my local, whether he had read my latest effort. 'Yes,' he replied, taking a steadying pull at his pot of Shep's, and then in a tone which implied that he was being very deliberately polite, 'Very good. I liked it'. He had another good swig at his beer and then went on, 'But I could hardly understand any of it. It's all those long words you use.'

So the label was put upon me, the label of the pretentious poseur. I promise Joe, in this book to avoid words like ethnogenealogical, and although anyone who goes into crossbreeding is entering the realms of biotechnology I will just call them dog breeders. On the whole I intend to stick to four letter words. Words like good and best – words which just about sum up longdogs as far as I am concerned.

This book is based upon personal experience of longdogs I have owned and worked, as well as a few first-hand accounts from close friends. Most of the ideas and observations are entirely my own and therefore can hardly be other than controversial. For this I make no apologies.

This book has not been written with the idea of being the last word on the origins and history of the particular breeds of longdog. It is, however, a practical book on the breeds, the various crosses, and their usefulness as hunting dogs.

A useful looking greyhound cross deerhound.

—1—

Why Longdogs?

WHAT IS A LONGDOG anyway? And what, for that matter, is a lurcher? Those old hands who are fortunate enough to have the genuine article can tell you, but the newcomer is often as not given so much contradictory advice that he is none the wiser. The lurcher is an *intentional* cross between a longdog and a herding dog, or the offspring of parents so bred. A longdog is either a purebred greyhound, whippet, deerhound, wolfhound, borzoi, saluki, Afghan or the less familiar Pharoah hound, Ibizan hound and sloughi, or a cross between two such purebreds, or the offspring of such until herding blood is introduced. My own definition of a longdog is a little bit wider than that of Ted Walsh's in *Lurchers and Longdogs* for whilst wholeheartedly agreeing with him that it includes the cross between two kinds of coursing dog, to me not only are the pure breeds themselves included, but also those dogs in the veins of which runs the blood of more than two types of longdog. In short, to my mind a longdog is one that carries no trace whatsoever of any blood other than longdog.

In his excellent book *My Life With Lurchers*, David Hancock states that he regards a lurcher as a cross between a collie and a greyhound which as a definition is a bit narrower than mine but none the worse for that. David's experience with the various types of collie/ greyhound is vast and there can be little doubt that he has bred many more of these animals, and on a sound scientific basis, than anyone else has in the past or probably will in the future. But where does this leave the cross between greyhound and retriever, so popular in East Anglia a few short decades ago? Or the whippet/Bedlington, which currently enjoys such well earned popularity? Or the Irish or Airedale cross greyhound, of which there were many in the north Lincolnshire of my youth? I will leave this one for the lurcher afficionados to sort out amongst themselves but perhaps it would be fair to say that the lurcher is an intentional cross between a longdog and a herding dog or terrier or working dog as defined by the Kennel Club.

There is, however, one word in the definition of a lurcher which I feel cannot be too heavily emphasised, and that word is *intentional*. Just as with terriers there are a tremendous number of lurchers about which are the unhappy result of random matings and should be called mongrels.

Why use a longdog?

Those who would wish to glean further information upon the subject of the currently popular collie/greyhound cross may be slightly disappointed in the contents of this book which is about a somewhat different article. Yet they may find something of interest, particularly if they are aware of some shortcoming in the canine they hoped would be the answer to every hunter's prayer, and this book may just provide the solution to their problem of choosing the most suitable dog for their needs.

If you should happen to be either the rather worried or, on the other hand, exceedingly elated possessor of what is sometimes described as 'a rabbit problem', then a lurcher of collie/greyhound breeding, could be the dog for you. From my own observations of them they require very little training, being natural rabbit catchers. With very little encouragement they may be relied upon to walk sedately at heel until they spot suitable quarry when, at a word or a sign from their owner, they will streak off after it, probably kill and return to station at heel, retrieving their catch in the process. In the unlikely event of their missing out on whatever they have pursued, they will simply return to heel empty-handed; the perfect catching machine. So what more do you require?

Well, in my own particular case, just a little bit more, or perhaps a better way of putting it would be to say 'a little bit different', what I want is a hunting not a herding dog. Whilst I would be the first to concede that the deerhound hybrids which I work, are neither so biddable nor so ready to go about their work in the same

10

The author's deerhound/greyhound waiting for a rabbit to bolt.

automaton-like way of the collie lurcher, they do, from my point of view, possess that little bit extra which makes them more interesting. One way in which I find the longdog differs from the collie lurcher is in its hunting as opposed to herding ability.

My own deerhound hybrids will hunt by sight and by getting their noses down. A great advantage as far as I am concerned, although were I only interested in lamping, as the last thing any lamper wants is for his dog to hunt by scent, the story would be a very different one. For hunting during the hours of daylight or at night without the aid of a lamp, deerhound hybrids take a deal of beating. All their senses are highly attuned and not only do they have good noses and superb hearing, but eyes like hawks in the daytime and like owls at night. Go out with a dog of this sort and it will very quickly become apparent that this is indeed so. Immediately it picks up any sort of scent, its ears swivel around like of couple of radar beacons for any sound of its quarry.

A longdog takes its quarry in a different way from the lurcher. There is a good deal less of the reflex action about them and more of the hunting. They have a quick look at the situation, size it up, work out the best way of coping with it and then carry on. Speaking

11

very generally indeed, I would not think that the score of a longdog, unless it were a very exceptional one, would ever approach that of a well-bred and well-trained collie lurcher on lamped rabbits, but on catching rabbits from ground cover, coursing hares (and I am not discussing lamped hares or, for that matter, coursed leverets, both of which I regard as utterly unsporting quarry), foxes under nearly any circumstances, and even larger quarry, longdogs will notch up a very nice tally, to which there must be added the attraction of seeing them at work.

A deerhound/greyhound stands stock still marking a rabbit in the reeds.

Unlike lesser canines, the closer that you are to your longdog, the closer it will be to you. You will find that your minds begin to function in a similar way, it like yours and yours like its and, as soon as this starts to happen, the magical door will be open to you. As a result of my association with these creatures over many years, I have become convinced that not only can the right sort of longdog, brought up within the confines of any normal household, understand just about every word that passes within that family's conversations but also they will get to a stage when they commence telepathy. This is where your mystical, as opposed to mythical, hounds come from. For there can definitely come into existence a bond, and a remarkably strong one, if you will but provide the ground and then give it a chance to develop. But to achieve this remember to keep to just one longdog and keep it in the house.

This all goes with the ability of the Celtic hound, be it deerhound, wolfhound, greyhound or hybrid, to work situations out. Anyone who gives one of them the opportunity to do this will be quite surprised by the manner in which these hounds can sum up just about any sort of situation, simple or complex, and then act upon it. Apart from more worthy considerations, this is one of the reasons why they are such consummate and exceedingly efficient thieves. By the time most of them are two years old, if they have been brought up as they should have been, inside their owner's house, they will have worked out how to open a door, including the door of your refrigerator in all likelihood, by then. This ability to reason will be dismissed by the so called experts in dog theory. 'Impossible,' they will say, 'All dogs, according to their ability, will learn to do all sorts of things, including some quite complicated ones, given the right sort of reward and punishment treatment.' They will, most probably, be quoting in so many words from one of the generally accepted manuals of instruction on the training of dogs, the most famous being by that outstanding German trainer of police dogs Colonel Conrad Most. I am in no doubt whatsoever that the Colonel is completely right in everything he advocates, *so far as the type of dog he is dealing with is concerned*.

In sheepdog bred lurchers the trainability and general willingness to please is there for all to see in the majority of these crossbreds. These characteristics would seem to stem from the collie portion of the mixture together, I would add, with a proneness to excitability and sometimes an over-developed sense of territorial jealousy which can be a problem when there are other dogs around. The greyhound blood will usually introduce a more phlegmatic type of animal although, of course, it is only too easy to over generalise in matters of this kind, but at the same time a good deal of the lurcher's reputation for craftiness and ability to thieve comes from the greyhound side of the breeding. It is sometimes stated, no doubt with the conviction of serious belief that no dog of any breed is capable of logical thought, that any behaviour has been conditioned by its training. Should anyone imagine this to be true, then I would advise them to pay a visit to the nearest greyhound track as soon as the opportunity presents itself. Whilst they are there, they can make a bet if they so desire, but the main object of their excursion should be to observe the manner in which various dogs run their races. They will very soon realise that there are

Two coursing greyhounds close on their hare.

certain dogs which not only figure out the best way to win, but which are also capable of working out the various situations as they develop.

This is one of the characteristics of the longdog which is all too frequently ignored and it is strange that there should be this misconception about the greyhound's IQ. Indeed, if one were to take the pronouncements of some of those in the collie bred lurcher camp too seriously, it would be only too easy to believe that the greyhound is some sort of over-muscled canine moron. Many of these persons are living in some sort of nostalgic cloud cuckoo land. Let's face it, the main ability of the sheepdog is to herd domestic animals, bringing them back to his master. This was a useful sort of attribute, from a hunting point of view, in the long gone days of hedges and gates on the farms of this country, when nets in general and the gate net in particular were such useful tools of the lurcherman's trade. The other attribute of the hunting dog, that of its empathy with the human, does not begin to come through until this is allowed to develop on a one man, one dog basis.

How often do we find this occurring? Not often, for many longdog owners are the lurcher show rosette hunters. I am unable to see either pleasure or profit in showing once anyone has decided to treat it as other than a bit of fun for a Sunday afternoon, but so many of them seem to be deadly serious about it all. Such people will usually have a string of two or three dogs at least, which they will exercise regularly in order the better to muscle them up, but never subjecting them to serious work in case they meet with some sort of injury. Other longdog owners are serious devotees of best of three hare killing contests, many of these taking place at the wrong time of the year so that either leverets, not yet versed in the wicked ways of the world, or pregnant does fall prey to their activities. Whilst I am quite certain that both of these forms of contest provide a very great deal of satisfaction and pleasure to those taking part in them, it does not seem to me to be a right and proper way of going about things. Neither are the owners and dogs likely to develop that special empathy that comes from hunting with a longdog.

I am quite sure that with all kinds of hunting dogs, the actual kind that is employed depends very much upon the temperament of its owner together with, of course, the reason for using it. Thus a man who happens to have a serious problem with rabbits and is more interested in pest control than sport will, in all probability, decide to use a good collie/greyhound cross and do most of his hunting at night on a lamp. Personally this is not my style, though whenever foxes attain pest-size populations, I tend to get rid of them by any means to hand, including taking them on a lamp at night, and, in pre-myxomatosis days, destroyed rabbits by any means possible including lamping. This was a long time prior to the invention of the lightweight battery which has enabled present day lamping to develop into such an efficient process, but I managed to make do with a vehicle-mounted spotlight. Before combine harvesters were used, the old reaper binder provided a very nice, short stubble over which one could drive with ease. I have also hunted with the aid of parachute flares from a two inch mortar but the game was not four footed and would provide the subject of rather a different book from this one. These days I am not faced by any quarry that has reached pest proportions and my only hunting is for sport and the pot. I therefore, run longdogs in preference to lurchers and instead of having by my side the, to my mind, almost mechanically behaving collie cross lurcher am accompanied by what I consider to be an animal with more character, which is a thinking type of hunter and, moreover one, which is often superior in its senses of sight, hearing and smell and is more an all round hunter rather than a specialised catching machine.

For either longdogs or lurchers to be of much use, they must be animals whose breeding is absolutely impeccable. I would not walk to the other side of the paddock to look at one of the grey-hound/whippet/Bedlington/collie/saluki/setter creatures which are so frequently advertised. Even in the unlikely event of the description being strictly accurate, there must be such a hotchpotch of genes present that the dog can turn out to be a very strange animal indeed. Without going into any long discussion on genetics basically the more breeds you mix together the worse the result is likely to be, both in looks and performance.

There is one matter which I feel cannot be stressed too strongly, That is should you intend to own and hunt with a longdog, then do just that and content yourself with one dog. All dogs, other than those intentionally hunted in packs, tend to perform better on their own and this is very true of the longdog, a creature of some strength of character. It will give a very great deal more satisfaction on a one man, one dog basis, and to have a kennel full is to merely make a burden for your own back. They are glamorous beasts though, and what could present a more romantic image, than two or three deerhounds, salukis or borzois on a leash? Should you merely wish to show them, all well and good, but if you want to hunt with them, and I fervently hope that this would be the case, I would suggest that you curb your enthusiasm and stop at one.

Heed my warning and not only will you make an obvious saving on food and vets' bills, but you will also find a true companion that is not too difficult to train and who will be capable of taking on just about any quarry you are likely to encounter. Have more than one longdog and, whilst at first everything may appear to be all right, it will not be long before you will be subjected to the sort of pack behaviour you least wish to experience.

Above all be very careful about working your longdog with terriers. It sometimes seems like quite a good notion; terrier bolting game from cover and longdog collaring it but, believe me, this is one of the best ways of ending up with a dead terrier. I must admit to hunting in this way myself sometimes and therefore am guilty of not practising what I preach, but, in mitigation, can only plead that I have been hunting for a great number of years and, hopefully, know just about how much I can expose one to the other. It is a practice against which I set my face for many years but recently have been given a very good terrier which, for once, seems to get on all right with longdogs, but it is not a way of doing things that I think I shall ever repeat. On the whole I think that it is true that if you are a hunting person, you are either a terrierman (woman) or not. If you are not leave terriers well alone.

A longdog class at a country show.

In recent years longdogs have tended to be less popular than the well-publicised collie lurchers, but there does seem to be a current resurgence of interest in them both as hunting and show dogs. During last summer at one or two country shows there were classes exclusively for longdogs, which attracted such breeds as greyhounds, deerhounds, salukis and borzois. These longdog classes attracted a fair amount of attention from the spectators, which was not surprising since the elegance and beauty of the dogs seemed only to be pushed into second place by that of some of their owners.

Greyhound.

Tunis '88

—2—

The Greyhound

I N THE MAKE UP OF any crossbred longdog it is more than probable that at least half will derive from the greyhound. Very frequently it will be a 50/50 mix that gives the best results, unlike the lurcher where half bred dogs are often not very satisfactory being a bit sluggish and in need of another helping of greyhound genes to speed up their performance a bit.

Just how long greyhounds have been on the go is not at all clear. Some say that they go back to the time of the Pharoahs – a couple of thousand years or so before the birth of Christ and that there are murals of them in the pyramids to prove it; others say that these are not greyhounds but salukis. It is rather like the affair of the Priest of Paris's hat; some say this and some say that. My own interpretation, for what it is worth since I am no sort of archaeologist, is that the dogs shown in the hunting scene from the tomb of Prince Senbi a Mer, which dates from about 2,000 BC, are from neither of these breeds, since they all seem to have prick ears. Pharoah hounds perhaps? Or is this too trite a suggestion? However, these animals were depicted at about the same time, as jackal-headed men so maybe they should not be thought of as realistic.

All these things being as they may, there does not appear to be much doubt that greyhounds of all sizes, as well as dogs resembling today's deerhounds, existed in Britain at the beginning of the 15th century for they are shown in one of the best sellers of the day *The Mayster of Game*, written by Edward, Duke of York. There are even earlier illustrations of them on the Bayeux Tapestry and they are mentioned in documents from the time of King John. They have always been highly prized animals and, as such, for the greater part of their history have only been available to those considered to be of sufficient rank and importance to merit such possessions. Since they are the archetypal hunting dogs, this would also indicate that the rich and exalted were somewhat given to the pleasures of the chase, and so it went on for many a long year.

But is this the case today? One may justifiably wonder. The answer seems to be in the negative – whilst much of the power in the land sits firmly in the anti-hunting lobby, a good many more of the powerful and wealthy are content to sit upon the fence. Whilst support for field sports seems to be on the increase amongst we of the lower orders, many of those at the top seem to regard such activities with an increasingly jaundiced eye.

Throughout the ages the greyhound has amply demonstrated his extreme versatility, the most recent example of this being when track racing was introduced as recently as 1926. The coursing dogs of the time took to it as a duck takes to water although even today there are odd ones who refuse to have any truck with the electric hare. Prior to this, however, the breed had shown to the full its capacity to deal with just about any sort of quarry from red deer to rat.

In early days the main quarry of the greyhound was deer and the hunting of these was the subject of a good deal of formality, but there was also other quarry of no mean stature in the shape of wolves and the formidable wild boar. Later on the hare became the main subject of the chase, just as it is today. At the other end of the scale, it is on record that in 1838 a ratting match took place between the famous ratting terrier, Billy and a greyhound. The two dogs tackled the rats on a basis of one dog at a time in the pit, its stint being to dispose of 100 rats in each instance. I should think that most of the money must have been on Billy and indeed he proved to be the winner killing his quota in six and a half minutes. However the greyhound proved himself no slouch at the job, finishing off his hundred in eight minutes, only 90 seconds behind Billy, one of the outstanding pit terriers of the age.

Incidentally, I always regard a spell of ratting as part of any hunting dog's education and one of the best ways of entering it to quarry. If ever you have a dog which strikes you as being a bit lacking in keenness, then let it have a go at a few rats. The less sharp

Two greyhounds in slips at Swaffham.

Widget Turner closes on his hare at Huntingdon.

it is, the more likely it is to be bitten with almost guaranteed improvement in performance. It would be just as well to be sure that its leptospirosis jabs are up to date though.

The show greyhound

There are in theory three sorts of greyhounds; track, show and coursing. Of these the show animals are of the least interest to us, unless, of course, we intend to go in solely for success at Cruft's and lesser dog shows. These are sometimes referred to as Cornish Greyhounds, the reason being that they were mainly bred and kept in Cornwall at one time. There must have been some reason for this but I have never been sufficiently interested in these representatives of the breed to try and find out. Probably, it was something similar to the inhabitants of County Durham's frenzied pursuit of the gigantic leek, or some lurcher men's determination to catch two more rabbits on the lamp than one of their friends: There is a certain magnificence about the show greyhound, turning the scale as it does at around 75lb and going up to as much as 30 inches in height. Unfortunately their appearance is just about all that they have to recommend them, As is to be expected of anything the fancy takes a liking to, these beautiful creatures are not a great deal of use for any sort of work. In order to satisfy the show requirements, abnormally deep chests together with tied-in elbows have been developed. Those dogs I have personally encountered have not been sufficiently muscled up to be of much practical use and, moreover, have seemed disinclined to show any interest in any sort of quarry. A sad testimony to the result of a preoccupation with producing show champions to the exclusion of all other considerations. Rosette hunters at lurcher shows please take note for this is the way in which you might easily find yourselves going, should you lose sight of the real purpose behind the keeping of a working dog.

Very few, if any, of the show-type greyhounds upon which I have briefly touched, are ever registered with the National Coursing Club and, therefore the majority of them are not eligible to take part in any coursing events or to race upon any greyhound racing track. More is the pity in some ways for this might just draw attention to the sorry plight of a certain, albeit infinitesimally small, section of the breed. At any of the lurcher shows I have been to I have never been aware of one of these king-sized, beautiful but utterly useless creatures being present but, I dare say, should the current vogue for showing lurchers continue it can only be a matter of time before the Cornishmen begin to put in their appearance.

Until this unhappy day arrives, let us forget about them and have a look at something a bit more worthwhile in the shape of the greyhound registered with the National Coursing Club as opposed to the Kennel Club.

The National Coursing Club

Any greyhound which is to take part in any track event under the rules of the National Greyhound Racing Club must, before it is eligible, have been registered with the National Coursing Club. Thus any dog which is to be used for track racing under Club rules, or which is to take part in coursing under rules, is subject to the National Coursing Club. The exceptions to such registration are the show greyhounds which I have briefly mentioned and dogs which are run on flapping tracks. Registration is strictly controlled and the system could, with benefit, be adopted by other breed societies. Under this system things can very occasionally go wrong but fraud is very difficult to perpetrate and the penalties are such as to discourage all but the most hardened miscreant. The National Coursing Club is a very well run organisation indeed and anything which can possibly be covered in the registration of offspring is never left to chance. The end result is the continuation of a breed of dog which has reigned supreme for several millenia and, thanks to the highly efficient efforts of the NCC, looks as though it will continue to bear the acccolade for a few more thousand years, apocalypse and nuclear disaster permitting.

The NCC registration of dogs destined for the track may seem to be something of a contradiction in terms but there is sound reasoning to support this way of doing things as well as reflecting the origins of track racing as a development from coursing.

Track and coursing greyhounds

Subtle differences in conformation occur between track and coursing dogs, although these are, in the majority of cases, not glaringly evident and indeed many track dogs do very well on the coursing field. There is also a fair amount of interbreeding between the two different sorts. In Ireland there is virtually no difference at all between the dogs which go in for the two sorts of sporting event. However, were I to be thinking about using a track greyhound for coursing under rules, I should be careful to select a fast but strong dog, paying particular attention to the feet and wrists, for a dog with any inherent weakness is unlikely to be up to the demands of running even the three rounds of an eight dog stake.

Two greyhounds turning their hare at Altcar.

Two top coursing greyhounds Lambert and Glatton General.

If one were crossing with another breed of longdog, say deerhound or saluki, one would expect to lose some of the greyhound speed but gain on stamina and would tend to select a greyhound that was physically sound, rather than one that was lightning fast to the first turn. Both the breeds of longdog I have mentioned are outstanding distance performers in their own right.

For lurcher breeding, one would be well advised to look for good temperament and conformation paying particular attention to the greyhound's feet and wrists and I would recommend good coursing stock for both these attributes, though there is no reason why you will not find the required conformation in a track bred dog, but you might just have to look a bit harder.

One thing I think should be borne in mind is that the minute a coursing dog starts to run a bit cunning, by which I mean standing off and letting the other participant in the course turn the hare into its ready and waiting jaws, its days as a coursing dog are over as it will not be picking up the points. Another way of looking at this is that just as soon as a coursing greyhound starts using a bit of sense, it is ready for retirement. Such is not so with the track dog. Anyone acquainted with the track will be abundantly aware that there are certain dogs which, in the way that they run a race, display marked intelligence and no small amount of wit and reasoning. Contrariwise to the coursing animal, this manifestation of the use of the grey matter is not immediately rewarded with compulsory retirement, but usually results in the brainy representative of the breed winning the race and these are the stock from which future generations will be bred. To perhaps slightly oversimplify the matter, track dogs are the better for employing their intellect, whilst coursing dogs are not encouraged in this respect and those coursing dogs that show a bit more intelligence by running cunning will be the best to use when breeding a longdog as intelligence counts when hunting.

For this reason, in my crossbreeding between greyhound and deerhound, I habitually use track dogs with a reputation for using their sense and that are stayers rather than sprinters, whenever I am looking for a stud dog. In this way I came across a local dog, a consistently good performer with a reputation of running a race with his head as well as his feet. Crossed with a strain of deerhound which, despite reports that this does not happen, was produced mainly with deerhound coursing in mind, it produced a strain of longdogs who, in physical ability and sheer cunning have proved the equal of any other type of crossbred running dog I have so far seen.

To return to the greyhound's place in the legitimate sporting scene, there has always been a certain amount of breeding of dual purpose track and coursing stock. These days, though it is much more the practice in Ireland than it is here in England – hence, probably, the popularity of Irish dogs which tend to be both fast and strong. There has been a tendency with English bred greyhounds for the coursing ones to be bred with too much emphasis on strength, as they may run four times in the day in a 16 dog stake and not enough on speed. The track ones on the other hand tend to be bred for early pace but with not enough consideration given to the physical attributes necessary to withstand the punishing demands of a coursing meeting, which is fair enough as on the track they only have to run once in the evening. Things were not always this way, however, and going back in time the outstanding track racing bitch, Burletta, the winner of the first greyhound Saint Leger, was the dam of both Genial Nobleman and Rotten Row, the winners of the Waterloo Cup in 1933 and 1937 respectively. There are also examples of track dogs doing extremely well in the coursing field, the outstanding example in my recollection being Mr Gocher's Endless Gossip which in 1952 won both the English Derby and Welsh Derby and then went on to getting very near to winning the Waterloo Cup.

This magnificent dog then went on to Cruft's where, appearing for the first time, he won in two classes in the face of animals which had been purposely bred for the show ring.

This all serves to demonstrate that in the greyhound, as in the whippet, we have an animal which has been bred not for appearance but for performance, although it goes without saying that its appearance has certainly not suffered in the process; this being amply illustrated by Endless Gossip's performance. This goes to prove the sense of selecting by performance and not other factors when breeding working dogs.

A good deal of thought and know-how has gone in to the breeding of the modern greyhound and there are quite a few instances of outcrosses being made in order to introduce various characteristics. The best known of these was, of course, in the 1770s when Lord Orford, in order to improve stamina, introduced bulldog blood – this being from the bulldogs of that time, a far cry from the travesty of a once proud breed which we see today upon the show bench. Credit for the strangest introduction, however, must surely go to Mr Dunn of Northumberland who in 1911 was, by resolution of the National Coursing Club, permitted to register in the Stud Book an Afghan hound by the name of Baz, which he had bought from an officer of the Indian Army, who in turn had acquired it from Pathan traders making their way through Baluchistan.

If you want a greyhound as a hunting companion then buy one as a six to eight week old puppy and bring it on as I suggest elsewhere in this book. You will be surprised by its intelligence and all round hunting ability if reared and trained correctly.

—3—

The Deerhound

T HE DEERHOUND HAS been with us for a very long time and records, including illustrations in the form of woodcuts are in existence dating back to the 15th century. In those days their appearance was much the same as it is today, a bit smaller and leaner perhaps, but a big, strong hound nevertheless, appreciably larger than the average greyhound of the time. In an early Scottish chronicle of 1526 there is an account of the theft of one of these dogs and feelings obviously ran high for, in the ensuing fight, no less than 160 men were left slain upon the field of battle. This gives some indication of the worth attached to these animals and might provide present day lurcher thieves with a bit of food for thought as an example of what may lie in store for them should the state of anarchy, which many of these people preach and sometimes practise, ever came about.

There can be little doubt that a similar sort of dog existed in Ireland at this time and, whatever the legends about such animals which were woven at a later date, the ancient hound of Ireland must have been something of this nature, despite the efforts of Captain Graham and others to produce something based on the deerhound although that little bit different. In all probability the deerhound of today approximates more to the ancient dog of the Celts than does anything else. This is exactly the sort of hound which would have been right for the control of wolves. In more modern times, whenever large and dangerous game is involved, this is the breed to which one naturally turns, either in its purebred form or crossed with the greyhound, another ancient breed. Australian kangaroo hounds as well as many of the American types of hunting dog rely heavily upon deerhound blood; this is not merely on account of their stature, speed and superb weatherproof coats, but also by reason of their general demeanour.

What a very great shame it is that such a superb type of working dog should be, as is the case with so many other breeds, in the process of being ruined by the desire to excel in the showring. All is not quite lost, however, for there still remains a small faction within the august circles of the Deerhound Club itself, who favour proving hounds in the field, not only in their native habitat of the Scottish Highlands but also, in the low fens of South Lincolnshire and North Norfolk, which is better hare coursing country.

I was fortunate enough to be offered a deerhound bitch by a very good friend of mine who for a number of years had run several of

Cloud a purebred deerhound bitch and marvellous worker.

this breed at most of the coursing meetings organised by the Deerhound Club. At the time he was in the process of reorganising his life a bit, and had arrived at the conclusion that he had one deerhound bitch too many. Whilst exchanging small talk with him in a local pub, I learned of this, and, when he went on to inform me that he was looking for a good home for the bitch, I was not long in offering to provide one. Thus I came to own a registered deerhound bitch, called Fly by me but registered at the Kennel Club under another name, of course. She had been bred by a lady whose primary and praiseworthy consideration was to breed sporting deerhounds with competitive coursing in mind. There is every likelihood that this particular bitch, would have just about fitted that description in every way. Bred from proven stock with a considerable helping of Miss Anastasia Noble's Ardkinglass strain very much in evidence she must have looked absolutely right when whelped and seemed like the answer to every sporting deerhound owner's prayer.

Alas, things can, and often do, go a bit wrong, and, in this case, the perfect female pup managed to be trodden on in the nest. At the time there was nothing much to show for this and, at eight weeks of age, she was sold in completely good faith. It was not until she reached the age to enter into competition that her physical condition manifested itself and she proved to be lame. No money was spared in veterinary fees, but X-rays showed that the femur had been fractured. Since the animal was but a few days old when this had occurred, the break had swiftly mended but, unfortunately, with a slight bend in this most important bone, just enough to cause a dislocation of the stifle whenever the bitch, who was by now developing a bit of substance, put any weight on the limb, as would have been the case whenever she was taking off or, more importantly, turning at speed. By the time I acquired her she was about three-years-old and, as a result of her disability, favoured her nearside hind leg to such a degree as to render her virtually three-legged. To someone like her owner, engaged as he was in competitive coursing, she had become something of a liability.

As soon as I became the owner of the bitch I took her along to all those veterinary practitioners whom I knew to be more than averagely sound on the ailments of sporting dogs, but, from all of them, received not one word of cheer. By this time she had reached about 26 inches at the shoulder, this being a couple of inches below the standard for bitches of this breed, but she was well muscled up and fit in every way apart, of course, from this tiresome injury. Despite her disabilities, the bitch was a good provider and, with her three sound quarters, was able to get along quite a bit faster than many other so called speedy dogs who were sound on all four. Her bodily condition apart, she was a cunning creature and could be relied on to painstakingly stalk her quarry, and to be in the right place at the right time when things were bolting.

Two deerhounds coursing in Lincolnshire.

My own veterinary surgeon, a very experienced man in whom I have absolute trust, advised me that there was a much higher than average chance of a chronic condition of arthritis forming in the joints of the injured limb, and, even when she was barely three years of age, it appeared to me that a condition of this nature was beginning to develop. Therefore, not seeing much of a lifespan before the unfortunate creature, I promptly decided to breed from her at the earliest opportunity. The time was fast approaching when I expected her to be coming into season and I started to examine the options that appeared to be open to me. In many of my previous stockbreeding activities the advice I had frequently followed with excellent results was: 'Breed pure'. This way of doing things always seemed to have payed off fairly well. I was getting identical advice in current circumstances. 'Breed pure,' they continued to advise me, 'And then you will discover you will be able to dispose of the pups at a far, far higher price than would be the case were they of mixed blood'. This all seemed to make good sense and those who were advising me were persons with plenty of experience not only in dog breeding, but also in dealing.

Easier said than done, however, and when it came to trying to put theory into practice, the story became a vastly different one. By reason of the bitch's demeanour I realised that matters were beginning to reach the point when decisions were going to have to be made and so I telephoned a very senior lady in the Deerhound

Club, of which at that time I was a fully paid up member, to ask whether she was able to assist me in the location of a suitable stud dog. I was immediately required to give chapter and verse about myself and this having been delivered, as I thought more or less satisfactorily, I was then asked to provide some details in respect of the bitch herself. These I gave willingly and, I think, reasonably fully, but, as I continued to say my piece, I became very aware that I was becoming less and less popular by the moment. The minute that I mentioned the kennel name, the reaction, which was quite obvious over the telephone, left me in very little doubt as to the outcome of the conversation.

'That's one of those from that coursing strain,' quoth the worthy dame to whom I had addressed my innocent inquiries. 'How tall is

A deerhound/greyhound bitch on the moors above Alnwick.

she?' she went on in an accusatory sort of tone. Becoming somewhat embarassed by now, 'Twenty-six inches,' I diffidently replied. What sounded remarkably like a stunned silence ensued. 'Better not breed from her,' my adviser continued. 'We don't want that sort of thing to be perpetuated. People who wish to go in for coursing should have coursing dogs, greyhounds and lurchers and that sort of thing.'

Feeling that little was to be gained from continuing the conversation, I politely thanked the lady for the benefit of her advice and rang off. This person, I may say, was one of the senior officials of the Deerhound Club which provided me with a pretty good idea of the general attitude prevailing within the inner councils of this august organisation.

So I took the advice which, I am quite sure was proferred with the best goodwill in the world, and went in for something other than deerhounds. But not much different. The good lady had mentioned lurchers. All right, then something of this nature it had better be, but not quite a lurcher – a longdog. This is how it came about that I breed the sort of stock which I go in for nowadays, and I can only say that I wish that I had gone in for them 50 years earlier.

Thwarted in my endeavours to produce pure bred deerhounds, I had to make my mind up rapidly as to what the next move should be. I had two options ready and open to me. About a mile from me was a breeder with several first rate border collies at stud, whilst 12 miles in the other direction I knew that the services of a first rate track greyhound would be available. I gave the matter as much thought as I could in the short time available to me and, after taking more than one look at my bitch, came down heavily in favour of the greyhound. It seemed to me that to put such a creature as her to anything less would be a very great pity. This is a move which I have never had cause to regret. On the odd occasions on which I visit Cruft's and listen to the accounts of how so many of the deerhounds have had their limbs pinned and plated, I am indeed thankful that I went the way I did. Also, having seen a few deerhound/sheepdog crosses, I am glad I did not proceed in that direction either. Those I have seen appear to be rather on the heavy side and many of them are rather more highly strung than I would look for in a dog.

My deerhound bitch had eight pups from this mating; these consisted of four dogs and four bitches. From the minute they were whelped they were completely outstanding. Six of them were black and two of them were brindle, the brindles being one of each, a

Two coursing deerhounds in slips.

bitch and a dog. The male was the strongest pup that I have ever encountered. Within an hour of being born, he had crawled over the top of his dam and dropped down at her back, making quite a lot of noise in the process. It was he I later named Grendel after the sea creature of the Nordic sagas, the one which gave Beowulf such a hard time of it. He was the largest whelp in the litter and has become an outstanding longdog. The other brindle in the litter was the smallest of them all. She had been booked before she was delivered, so to speak.

A friend had mentioned to me, as soon as she knew that these pups were on the way, that she would be interested in a brindle bitch and one had been promised to her sight unseen. She was Jane Hilden's well known Jessica I and anyone who has attended lurcher shows anywhere in the south of England will not need to be reminded of her. In her first two years of showing she won 57 awards and then went on and on in the same vein. Not just a pretty face either, but a first rate working bitch as well. She was taking all sorts of quarry and taking them well by the time that she was two-years-old. Alas, the gods take whom they love, and she had to be put down as a result of an injury by the time she was five.

I kept another bitch for myself from this litter, one which, from the viewpoint of conformation, could, I think, have slightly had the edge on Jessica, and, just to prove this assertion, I would mention

Jane Hilden with Jessica.

that I have only ever put her into a lurcher show on one occasion. It was on a wet Sunday afternoon when my son-in-law Mick Broad and I were at something of a loose end and there being a lurcher show just down the road from us at Waltham, we decided to pay it a visit. My entry was to put it bluntly not well groomed and I had not even bothered to brush off traces of dried mud, not being very much bothered about appearances since I regard all lurcher and terrier shows as merely being a bit of fun. My bitch just happened to pip Jessica at the post, which was quite satisfying to me if not Jane Hilden.

None of the bitches from this litter have been bred from, which is a shame. I really must do something about this before it is too late. Although Gudrun, the one that I kept, is rising seven-years-old, it is not too late, for longdogs can start off their breeding life at a greater age than this without much in the way of problems. One thing is for certain, I want nothing but longdog blood. Grendel has sired quite a few litters, mainly to lurcher bitches, where there is not a shadow of doubt that he has left his mark in an unmistakable way. The very first bitch he covered was a border collie, which came of working stock from a hill farm in Scotland. I cannot say that any of the resulting litter when mature were to my liking and I had all my prejudices confirmed concerning the collie/longdog hybrid. For me, many collie crosses are a bit too nervy and jumpy to be endured, and I do not much care for their habit of trying to herd everything they encounter.

Why do I favour the deerhound hybrids? Whilst the purebred deerhound can be a bit on the ungainly side, this seldom seems to come through in the crosses, although, if it is going to do so, in my experience it nearly always appears in the males of this breeding; I have yet to see it in any of the females. In any case, I am not very keen about male dogs for hunting, much preferring bitches which I have found to be keener, easier to train and rather more inclined to be natural hunters. That is not to say that there are no males which are good at the job; this would be far from the truth, but the females are more dependable in this respect. Should you find yourself with one of the, to my mind, slightly overlarge male deerhound hybrids, you will probably end up with a big, strong sort of dog, quite fast and quite amenable. Maybe it will be a bit slow on the turn, but it will probably have stamina to go on for a very long time and therefore, as a hare or fox dog be quite a good performer. In any case, it will probably have a pleasant disposition and will be amenable to lead training, so you can take it around with you, should you wish to cultivate the macho image. It will knock over the odd rabbit, probably lamp as well as a good many others and not be much of a problem to train to stock of all kinds. You will, with very little doubt, have all manner of weird characters around who will offer you what they consider to be princely sums for it, or even endeavour to steal it. Have no truck with these sorts, for they will have in mind the pursuit of, at best, fallow and roe, and, at worst, sheep and its existence will, in all likelihood, be a pretty miserable one with the unfortunate beast taking its rest amongst heaps of scrap iron.

As I have mentioned, the bitches from the straight greyhound/ deerhound cross are fairly certain to grow out right, reaching about 26 inches in height and turning the scale at around 60 pounds; pretty near ideal for all sporting purposes, in fact. Compact enough to turn with a rabbit, and with speed and stamina enough to take a hare. Of all the single-handed hare catchers that I know, most of these have either deerhound or saluki blood in them, but we are discussing the deerhound now and I will have more to say of the saluki, later on in the book.

A good greyhound/deerhound hybrid, once it develops the knack, (and it will not take very long in the majority of cases, although perhaps receiving a few chops to start with) is well capable of taking and killing a fox without much assistance. A timely word of warning, however – by the same token, such a dog, able and willing to annihilate foxes, is equally adept at taking out another dog and this is a tendency for which one must be on one's guard. As far as my own dogs are concerned, they have shown a marked dislike for other dogs on occasions and while they do not go so far as to attack them I do not think they would require very much encouragement to do so. Although labelled by some quite well-known and highly regarded lurcher owners as being difficult to train, such has not been my own experience.

I think the first cross to be the right one for, by breeding to three-quarters in either direction, it is easy to upset the balance. A dog which is three-quarter deerhound will be found to be pretty near straight deerhound and similarly if it is three-quarter greyhound. The two breeds have a fair amount in common and this will assert itself in anything beyond the straight cross bitch, so that it will be necessary to be rigorous in one's culling of the resulting litter for many genetic factors will have been brought into play and there will be pups which are both physically and genetically almost pure greyhounds and pure deerhounds. But then rigorous culling should form part of any serious stock breeding programme from camels to white mice. With all due respect to that doyen of the sporting scene, Phil Drabble, I would tend not to place too much importance upon his version of the three-quarter bred deerhound in that very informative and exceedingly readable book of his, *Of Pedigree Unkown*. My own opinion is that the title of the book is a good deal more indicative of what he got from his scrap iron merchant friend than what these dogs were purported to be.

A deerhound cross closing on its rabbit.

So, let us assume that you either breed or otherwise come by that often advertised, but difficult to find article, the genuine hybrid greyhound/deerhound, and I will make no apologies for reiterating the word, Genuine giving it a captial letter this time, for there are a fair few of the other sort around. Where do we go from here? You should forget about taking your wife or your girlfriend out for the day every weekend or forget about being out with the boys, living it up all the time, for you now have a full-time commitment. You should dismiss entirely any ideas that you may be entertaining regarding your trip to the Costa Brava or Majorca or Greece or Turkey or Bangkok, for you have a job on your hands. You have become a hunter, the committed owner of a hunting animal of great potential and, as such, are subject to a regime which, whilst not exactly onerous, is nevertheless tying.

A deerhound/greyhound cross greyhound/whippet.

When at last you have managed to train this animal and subject it to your will, and once it has started to get into the habit of doing the things you want is to do, you may relax, for it is unlikely to forget them. But slip up, neglect or be slipshod in your initial training routine, and you may as well not have bothered to start it. This is a professional hunter's dog, one which, if you do your job correctly, will be an animal par excellence, such as in your wildest dreams you would have never imagined having, but this will be at the expense of hard working days and sleepless nights and a certain amount of self-deprivation. That is, of course, if you are anything other than an utterly dedicated longdogman. And I don't mean lurcherman.

To the dyed-in-the-wool longdogman, the dedicated operator of such creatures, life will not be so hard or, perhaps, it may just not seem so hard, for the understanding of this unique sort of canine mind will be there. This is the breed of man or woman, who lives, sleeps, eats and generally exists with his or her hound, regarding it as part of the ongoing general scene.

Deerhounds and their hybrids are different, however, as you will soon discover should you have them in the house with you as well as other dogs. They will usually remain aloof from these and, should your other breeds tend to congregate close to you, your deerhound will probably remain aloof from you as well. Whilst they will be glad to see you should you have been away for a short while, you will be unlikely to receive the effusive welcome shown by a collie, not to speak of the hysterical reactions of the spaniel or the terrier, for deerhounds are not as other dogs. Just as the homicidal maniac in some cases possesses an extra chromosome, so, I think, may this sort of longdog, which seems to have some different balance within its genes unlike other dogs. Not that it is the homicidal chromosome, thank goodness, in a dog of this ability and power. They are, quite simply, different from the rest of the canine tribe and, for this reason if for no other, their training and indeed general regime of management should not be quite the same as that afforded to other dogs. These animals, given the opportunity, will work out a situation in a manner which it is extremely unlikely that you will ever find any other sort of dog capable of doing.

—4—

The Saluki and Afghan

Afghans

I HAVE NOT THE slightest hesitation in stating that the Afghan hound that I owned was the most brainless and intractable animal I have ever had. I use the word, 'animal', advisedly, for all the pigs that I have ever bred were considerably more intelligent, and I think the same goes for most of the sheep which have passed through my hands. Sheep will, at any rate, come when called if they are aware that food is in the offing, but my Afghan hound would not even do this. It was quite impossible to train it off of livestock and, whenever the thing saw the slightest chance of running away, it would take it, compounding its iniquity by forgetting in which direction its home lay and requiring a full-scale search to find it. A beautiful dog and with a very sweet disposition but, so far as anyone could see, not a brain in its long elegant head. I and other experienced dog handlers spent hours endeavouring to encourage it to respond to the simplest of commands without the glimmer of the slightest degree of success. It would not come when called, whistled at, or signalled to, even though I was making myself hoarse, breathless and stiff in the joints while invitingly dangling half a pound of best steak in front of the creature's nose. It was fortunate that I was living in Ireland at the time for people there are more tolerant of canine idiosyn-cracies, as well as there being more space out of doors and less traffic, so stray dogs stand more of a chance of survival than would be the case in England.

One of this dog's more tiresome escapades was to run off after some sheep which were peacefully grazing and minding their own business on some land at Macgilligan Point which was situated alongside what was a military firing range at the time. The red flags were up, the armoured cars were on the firing range and the Besas were aimed towards the targets, when, into their sights must have erupted half a dozen sheep with a hairy, mentally defective creature lolloping after them with me in hot pursuit. 'Get off the bloody range', yelled a stentorian Army-type voice. 'Shoot the blasted thing and be done with it', I yelled back in probably equally strident tones. 'Can't. I might hit the sheep', came back the reply, followed by more abusive advice, the subject of which was both the dog, myself and a good many of my predecessors. Fortunately they held their fire. They must have been tempted not to do so.

By this time all the sheep, bar one, had been lost somewhere in the chase and the dog was pursuing this solitary ewe round and round a small concrete pillbox which looked as though it had been left over from 1939–45. For some reason or other, perhaps it had become dizzy, the sheep suddenly reversed its course and, instead of going round the blockhouse in a clockwise direction, started going round it anti-clockwise. This could only have one result, of course – a head on confrontation between dog and sheep. I rushed towards them, the wild cries of the mechanised cavalarymen ringing in my ears. Were they cheering me on? No, they were not. At any rate, I thought, once it starts to worry the sheep, I can collar it, but there was no necessity for me to do so, for, as soon as the wretched hound spotted the sheep coming towards it, it fled from the animal and galloped back to me as fast as its legs would carry it with a 'Save me! Save me!' sort of expression on its stupid face. I had it on a lead in a trice and made good my departure as rapidly as was possible, pursued by the oaths of the lads in khaki.

Shortly after this episode I discovered that yet another drawback existed, this time in the shape of its long, silky coat. Yet again it managed to escape from home and, as could have been forecast, lost itself, this time turning up on the doorstep of a farmer I knew slightly and who lived some two or three miles away. He telephoned and informed me where it was and I went round to his place straight away to get it, to find that he had shut it up in an old pigsty while he offered me a helping of Irish hospitality. This concluded, I was in the process of collecting the dog from its temporary lodging, when the farmer said; 'Might be as well if you kept your eye on the dog, for the last lot of pigs I had in there was

An ice-cream was about the only thing my Afghan could catch.

Note the very necessary lead and restraining hand.

lousy. He might just be taking a bit more away with him than he came with.'

Sure enough, his prognostication was not an emtpy one, the thing was well infested. 'Benzyl benzoate', thought I, 'That's the stuff for lice.' Indeed it is, and its also the stuff for mange and human scabies and other nasties of this nature. But where to purchase some? I knew all the shopkeepers in the small town near where I lived and did not want them to be putting two and two together and making five, for they would immediately reach the conclusion that my children were suffering from pediculosis or scabies or something of that nature. I therefore went to another town, some 40 miles away and, going into the first chemist's shop I saw, asked to be supplied with the required remedy. Now Afghans are large dogs and have copious coats, so I asked for a good helping of the stuff, about a litre. 'Sure, there's a big family you would be having', said the good-natured pharmacist as he dispensed the medicine. It so happened that the town to which I had gone had recently had a University started up there, and, as I turned away from the counter with my purchase, there was the undergraduate daughter of one of my worthier and snootier neighbours standing next to me and taking in the entire conversation. Some you can't win.

I went to a job in West Africa and one of my farming acquaintances offered to have the dog whilst I was over there. When I returned his family had become so attached to it that they asked if they might keep it. It was still as intractable as it always had been, I heaved a sigh of relief and swiftly agreed. That was over 20 years ago and perhaps it is still going strong, chasing sheep under the muzzles of the guns and becoming infested with lice.

Well, so far there has not been much about salukis, perhaps, but salukis have coats of differing lengths, depending upon their place of origin, and all an Afghan is, is the longest-haired saluki of the lot, having, no doubt, grown a covering of this length as protection against the Himalayan snows. Those who breed Afghans will tell you how they are used in Afghanistan and the neighbouring territories in the pursuit of dangerous prey – leopard being the main quarry mentioned. Well, having witnessed the performance of my Afghan when confronted with a vertigo-stricken sheep at Macgilligan, my money would not be on one of these when matched against a leopard. Entertaining the opinion I do of their abilities, I was interested to see in *The Field* some years ago a letter from a retired senior army officer who said that, when he had been a young subaltern on the Frontier some 50 or 60 years previously, he had encountered several of these dogs at various times. They had not been hunting leopard or wolves or bear or even any of the non-dangerous creatures which occur there, but had been used as some sort of guard dogs around the sheep and goats. One part of his correspondence stuck in my mind; 'Some of the brutes could be quite savage,' he wrote, 'And one soon learned for what purpose the Officer of the Day at Landi Khotal was required to carry a sword.' Having had the experience I have of the Afghan hound, I am well prepared to leave the last word regarding them with the gallant Major-General (Retd.).

Salukis

Some people speak quite highly of salukis, others not so highly, but all the people I talk to seem to have one thing in common, which put me in mind of a rather weak joke which was the last word in schoolboy humour when I was about seven-years-old; it went something like this:

Teacher: Now, Johnny, give me a sentence containing the word 'seldom'.

Johnny: My father had some rabbits but he selled 'em.

End of funny story, but I was reminded of it when I asked people for their experiences concerning salukis. A number of those I asked had had one, or in some cases more than one, but had selled 'em. There must have been some reason for this I reasoned, and pursued my investigations further, asking friends and relatives of theirs why this had happened. The ultimate reason seemed to be that they had, each and every one of them been impossible to train off livestock. This rang a bell; it was the story of my Afghan over again.

I decided to start at the beginning. There can be little doubt that all longdogs must share some sort of common ancestry but their separate breed evolution must have commenced thousands of years ago, the various types, in the meantime, adapting themselves to whatever happened to be their particular environment. Dogs of the greyhound type seem to have been the subject of natural selection in Europe, dividing and outbreeding to become the greyhounds, deerhounds, borzois and so on as we know them today, each of them becoming adapted to their particular location and to whatever quarry it mainly pursued. The Asian counterpart of the European greyhound types must have been the ancestor of today's salukis, Afghans and sloughis. The odds are that, in its original form, it resembled today's saluki, evolving into the other varieties to suit differences in climate – the smoother haired types appearing in the more arid deserts and the longer haired sorts in the higher, wetter and cooler parts. When this actually happened is so long ago as to be lost in the mists of time but it certainly occurred before the era when the Egyptians became engaged in the construction of pyramids for there, for all to see, painted on the walls of the sepulchral chambers within these structures are representations of hounds which appear to differ very little from the salukis of today.

A saluki/greyhound.

Coming a bit closer to our own time, a dog of saluki type is depicted upon Greek vases of the fifth and sixth centuries, and, proceeding in history a good deal further forward, dogs of this breed are shown in the Renaissance paintings of Veronese and, also of this period, on a very beautiful bas-relief which was executed for Cosimo de Medici by the famous Florentine silversmith Benevenuto Cellini. This evidence would indicate that the saluki must have been well established throughout the Near and Middle East as well as the seaboard of the Mediterranean, becoming so widespread as to assume different forms dependent upon the geographical location. Not only do these tend to differ from one another in the degree of hairiness as has already been touched upon, but also in colour, the darker coloured dogs being more likely to occur in the northern parts of their habitat, in the area of what has now become Syria, and the lighter coloured ones, which also tend towards smoother coats, appearing in the more southerly regions, reaching the limit of their natural homelands in Saudi Arabia. Those who have had experience with the breed seem to be of one mind that the lighter coloured, smoother coated types tend to be more intelligent than the darker, hairier sorts.

The breed was not represented at all in this country until about a century ago when returning travellers from the East started to bring the odd one back with them. But it was not until 1897, when the Honourable Florence Amherst started to breed them, that they became at all well-known in this country. The Kennel Club did not recognise the breed until the 1920s. Of very elegant appearance, one has very little difficulty in realising why the saluki has proved to be so attractive to its band of fanciers.

The saluki itself, and in its crosses with the greyhound, can be a very fast dog, moreover a dog which is possessed of a considerable degree of stamina. As a result of this they have become very popular with the 'best of three' hare coursing fraternity. Unkind critics of the breed have, upon occasion, alleged that the reason they can keep on going for so long is because they never really try. I feel that this comment on the breed is not altogether justified. If you are coursing a hare, the way in which the dog goes about the job must depend upon whether you wish to kill the quarry or to pick up points whilst coursing under rules. The dog which is steadier but keeps going longer will do better at catching its hare, but the one with all the dash will score better when coursing under rules. As with lurchers, so with longdogs, it is very much a matter of 'horses for courses'.

On their native heath, or rather native desert, salukis are used in the coursing of gazelle and sometimes the desert hare. Usually they are run as a pair at the former quarry and singly at the later. The pursuit of the gazelle is sometimes assisted by a trained falcon which has been conditioned to attack the head of the prey. This must be about the most romantic form of hunting that it is possible to find. Arab steeds, elegant hounds, falcons and flowing robes – a far cry from the British coursing scene with a fair amount of mud, thick weather-proof garments and, now and then, some funny looking dogs, which, despite their appearance, are good at knocking up the points. However, the Arabian Nights effect is all very well but must be a bit harder on the dogs than the Fenland soft going, which is why the saluki is a very hard dog with such strong bone and good feet. The rocks and stones of the Eastern desert has seen to that for injuries must be frequent and none but the fittest survive. At the same time much the same can be said in favour of the deerhound so long as it is from good coursing stock. Neverthless, from the point of view of having a hard sort of animal with the ability to keep going for a long course in difficult conditions, a saluki would seem hard to beat. Other considerations exist, however.

That these dogs do not always seem to try very hard is, in some instances, correct but it is fairly easy to see why this should be so. In their native deserts there is little chance of the quarry escaping for there are no hedges for it to go through, no main roads to cross and no electrified railways in the way. All involved can thus keep on going as long as their stamina allows them to. The barley prairies of East Anglia and Salisbury Plain are the nearest we have to this open environment and salukis may be expected to acquit themselves well when being run at hares in these areas. The localities to which I refer also resemble the desert in yet another way in that neither the arable prairies of Norfolk and Suffolk, nor the empty regions of Arabian deserts are exactly overpopulated with farm livestock, particularly sheep, in the presence of which these dogs can be an unmitigated pest. It might just be possible to train them off stock, if they were reared on a farm where there were a great many sheep but, even in these circumstances, I would expect the average longdog trainer to have his work cut out. I don't know whether the Duke of Beaufort's recommended cure might do the trick. This, should you not have heard of it, is to secure the dog in a narrow passage and run a flock of sheep over the top of it. It works pretty well, should the dog survive, but always presupposes that you have a handy flock of sheep at your disposal. Domestic fowl pose similar problems without the benefit of any sort of suggested remedy.

There might not be quite so many difficulties of this nature were the dog to be brought up from a very early age in an environment where there already were domestic animals. In fact one of the few persons I know who swears by salukis rather than at them has a smallholding in Sussex where everything on the place is brought up cheek by jowl. Mind you, his are the short haired, smooth coated variety, which are inclined to be more biddable than the longer haired sorts; in fact, a rule of thumb with salukis might be that the longer the coat the more difficult the dog. This problem in respect of livestock militates against salukis ever being much use as an all round dog but, should one merely be contemplating the prospect of winning a bob or two in 'best of three' hare killing contests over the right sort of country, then they certainly have their place in the scheme of things.

Any sort of dog which is of unsatisfactory temperament when in the presence of farm and domestic livestock is not only a constant

A saluki being slipped on a hare.

source of embarassment from both the social and financial viewpoints but also an unremitting focus of anxiety. A lady who lives not far from me is an extremely competent breeder and trainer of both Bedlingtons and whippets and Bedlington/whippet crosses. She takes a great deal of trouble with them and is meticulous in her selection of the right sort of breeding stock which she has acquired regardless of expense and trains her dogs to a very

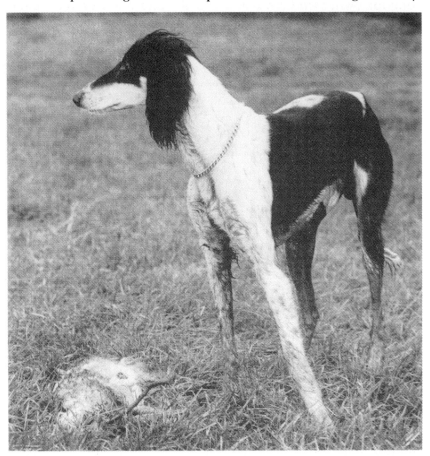

Some salukis will retrieve.

high standard. Her hitherto unblemished record was marred only when her husband acquired a pair of salukis which, despite her skills, she was unable to break to livestock. This resulted in their attacking a flock of sheep, saddling her with swingeing fines and heavy damages.

So whatever your other feelings in the matter may happen to be, I would suggest that, should you be intent in going in for this breed, you should make absolutely certain that whatever housing you keep them in is completely secure. Then, before slipping them, just have a good look around to ensure that there is no form of farm livestock anywhere nearby.

Should you happen to be one of those comparative rarities – a longdog owner who ventures forth alone with but a single hound, unlike the more usual type who does not feel himself adequately turned out without at least three dogs towing him along, closely followed by at least one friend similarly equipped (or should I say impeded) – there may just be a chance for you with a saluki. Should you also happen to be a whiz at dog training you may have a chance but, even then, be very wary whenever you slip your pride and joy within half a mile of any grazing stock. A friend of mine, who I reckon to be the best longdog and lurcher trainer that I have ever met, came by two salukis of the short haired variety. He acquired them at an early age and, as I say, he is something out of the ordinary with longdogs. They were as alike as two peas in a pod in appearance but this is where the resemblance came to an end for they were almost diametrically opposed in temperament. One of them responded to training in a satisfactory way, it obeyed all the usual commands and was safe with stock; its fellow was a most unbiddable sort of beast, would not return when summoned and ended its days by running away, whilst being exercised, and bolting beneath the wheels of a car, thus proving how unpredictable their behaviour can be.

Mind you, the last thing I would wish to exhibit would be any form of prejudice or bias and, although one's own gut-feelings seldom, if ever, in my experience seem to lead one very far astray so long as one has the courage to pursue one's convictions, I determined to seek the reactions of as many other people as I could, people who might have had any sort of experience of these very decorative Oriental canines.

With this foremost in my mind, I sought out a lady whom it should not be too difficult to identify for she is a Master of Hounds of many years standing. This sprightly octogenarian, who still goes out with her beagles in the same way she did before the First World War is, in my estimation, one of the finest sources of any information whatsoever on all matters both canine and equine. Without, I hope, giving the game away to too great an extent I inquired of the Master whether she had at any time had any experience of salukis. 'I have indeed,' quoth she. 'I well remember a brother of mine, who was a keen coursing enthusiast, acquiring two such dogs.' I immediately became all ears and requested the next instalment of the saga. This was not long in coming and it transpired that the Master's brother, having heard of the fabulous performances of these dogs, somewhere back in the 1920s when they were beginning to become established in this country, arranged a greyhound versus saluki coursing event.

The hare was set up for the first course and all those present stood in eager anticipation of what was about to take place. It proved to be something of an anti-climax when the greyhound rapidly got on terms with the hare followed by the saluki which cantered along behind them. 'Well; better luck next time,' they thought and set about getting the next item on the programme under way. This, of course, was down to the remaining saluki and the other greyhound. Optimistically hoping for something with a little more action to it this time, the spectators stood by with bated breath. Both dogs were slipped at the opportune moment and the greyhound smartly got under way. Having laid off nicely for a short space in order to size up the situation, he swiftly got to his hare and, after making a few passes, killed. Again, in this bout, the saluki seemed content to go along for the sake of taking the exercise. In fact the exercise must have assumed important proportions with it for, completely ignoring the fact that the greyhound was killing the hare, the saluki simply kept going and was very soon afterwards seen for a moment as it disappeared over the skyline into the great blue yonder from which it did not deign to reappear until the sun was setting, not, one would have thought to howls of the wildest approbation.

I next went to a friend of mine who is the owner of two very useful and very successful track greyhounds as well as some handy coursing deerhounds which he has run at various meetings arranged by the Deerhound Club. In answer to my inquiries he informed me that he had indeed witnessed salukis in action and that they were being run over a bleak stretch of open mountainside in northern Scotland. This had been at an event jointly organised by the Deerhound Club and the Saluki Hound Club. The coursing events had been run alternately between first two deerhounds and then two salukis. The deerhounds had performed in a way that showed them to their best advantage in their native habitat, but it seemed that the contribution the salukis were able to make to the proceedings was anything but perfect. A pair of them were run at a hare; one of them killed and the other, perhaps in some sort of a state of frustrated chagrin, took off on its own. It paid no heed to the cries of its owner to return to him and so he set off in pursuit of the thing. He was rewarded for his efforts by the dog allowing him to approach to within some few yards of it, before taking off again, only to repeat the entire process every few hundred yards. Hound and owner were last observed departing into the sunset somewhere behind Daviot Moor.

Following publication of the first edition of this book, I received a letter, which I feel that in all fairness I must mention, from a gentleman in the North of England, who believed himself to be the owner of the dog described in the preceding paragraph. He tells me that, of 24 salukis which took part in the three day meeting at Daviot, this was the only one of their number which behaved in this manner. He goes on to say that over the past few years at similar meetings, he met with only three salukis which were not biddable and which did not return to hand after coursing. This was out of fields of up to 32 hounds, which, say, over a hypothetical period of three years would indicate an infinitesimally small percentage of salukis which do not return to hand when required to do so, a score which I cannot say is borne out by my own observations.

Someone else, an experienced longdog, lurcher and terrierman, to whom I addressed my inquiries, told me that he had for a time been the owner of two salukis. Of these, one would come when it was called but the other behaved in a manner to indicate that it was stone deaf at such times. He had eventually rid himself of both of them. I asked why he had parted with the obedient one, it being abundantly obvious why he should have sent the other one on its way. Of all the examples of which I was aware this one was one of the few which seemed in any way ready to accede to its handler's requirements, most of them demonstrating no desire to please or even effect some sort of compromise.

'I had to get rid of it for it had a jinx on it,' said he. As we continued to discuss the matter, enlightenment commenced to dawn upon me. This must be the dog, known locally as 'The Accident'. A fast dog and a good stayer, it possessed the added attraction of sometimes doing what was required of it, but it also had the appalling reputation of bringing death and destruction to all about it. This was first manifest when the car in which it had been travelling had become involved in a traffic accident which had resulted in the death of another dog. Soon after this unfortunate happening, its owner had let it out in order the better to demonstrate some part of its conformation to a friend who was paying him a visit. Whilst so engaged, another of his dogs ventured unsupervised upon the road and was mown down by a passing vehicle. Being a bit superstitious, he had immediately rid himself of the animal, which, since then, has changed hands on several occasions, leaving a trail of canine mayhem in its wake.

Its kennel companion, incidentally, was cast in an entirely different mould, one which more properly seemed to fill the saluki role. It possessed no Jonah-like qualities, insofar as I am aware, and never put a hex on man or beast, merely driving its owner well nigh out of his mind by what seems to be the usual characteristic of the breed, mainly evidenced by an unwillingness to return to its owner, whether summoned or not. In utter desperation, not unmingled with frustration, on one particular occasion its owner was endeavouring to exercise it in the middle of a 40 acre arable field, which, this being in the middle of winter, had been deep ploughed and the soil was strong, holding clay of a particularly glutinous nature. Having come to the end of all attempts to deal with the beast in any sort of a reasonable way, he removed one of his wellies and flung it at the dog which, at this moment, was doing one of its usual tricks of standing off at some four or five yards and not only sulkily failing to come when it was called but also retreating whenever it was approached.

As is so frequently the case when in the grip of powerful emotion, (murderous intent in this case), my informant's aim was other than true and the boot, although propelled with a good deal of feeling as well as strength, failed to connect as had been the intention. The matter did not end there, however, for the dog, perhaps receiving some sort of message that something or other was required of it, picked up the makeshift projectile and did not retrieve it to hand but proudly carried it off into the next field, leaving its would-be trainer to return home as best he could in the vile wintery weather with one frozen foot.

These were the first salukis that he owned and, one scarcely needs to add, they were the last. I would just reiterate that this man is a very experienced and highly skilled trainer of all manner of hunting dogs, by no means one of your 'keep it if you like it, flog it if you don't' breed of dog owners.

So, from my point of view, it begins to look as though it is very much the case that, should you become the owner of a saluki, it may be fairly difficult for you to have any chance of winning. Money you may win in best of three hare killing contests, always providing that these take place in the right environment, pitting your dog's abilities against others of like sort. Should this be the way in which you can obtain a degree of satisfaction from the longdog, all well and good, but personally, I look for a closer relationship with a dog than can be provided in this way.

One thing, however, has become abundantly clear to me during my researches into the saluki and that is very occasionally one may be found which is outstandingly excellent in every way, but it also seems that one will become the possessor of such a canine paragon solely by chance. And yet I just wonder; there are those who have taken these dogs, frequently rescue jobs, and made a success of them. They are almost habitually people with a very real empathy with hunting dogs and there may exist some sort of sympathetic skein which makes one man a successful and satisfied saluki owner, leaving all the rest of us with very little opinion of the breed at all. There are certain satisfactions about approaching one's dotage and one of these is that one can justifiably come to the conclusion that one is too old to try out various things that, had one been younger, might have offered the sort of challenge which one could not in all fairness to oneself ignore. I am glad to be in that category where I no longer need to have a go with a saluki just in order to prove to myself that I am utterly incapable of dealing with it.

—5—

The Wolfhound and Borzoi

The Wolfhound

HAVING CUT MY teeth, so to speak, with whippets, pressing business on the Continent and North Africa between 1939 and 1945 kept me from having any dogs for a few years, but soon after this I found myself hunting with an Irish wolfhound. It had been left in my charge by an acquaintance who was leaving the district to take up other employment, as the governor of a prison. This was in Africa during the time of Mau Mau when a number of such establishments had to be built in a hurry. Such was the speed with which everything had to be organised that he was having to take up residence in some sort of temporary accommodation (probably a tent) and had no means of housing or looking after the dog. Since I was taking over from him the running of a 24,000 acre ranch, I seemed to be the obvious person to have the animal for the time being.

We had dogs of our own and so one more made little difference, particularly since there was a large influx of zebra, the numbers of which had to be reduced to such an extent that even after the Turkana labour and I had taken our portions, there was still enough meat left over to have provisioned a pack of foxhounds, let alone my mini bobbery pack. So I agreed to his proposal that I should have Warwick for a time. Quite apart from helping the chap out, I must admit that any dog which is an unknown quantity immediately interests me and, in this case, I strongly desired to

59

explore the hunting capabilities of the beast. The reputation of Irish wolfhounds was and still is that they are not much good as working dogs, but I wished to discover whether this really was so, and there could be no better chance of putting matters to the test than in my current situation: I had getting on for 40 square miles of completely unfenced, undeveloped African bush at my disposal which, moreover, carried a very large amount of game.

Warwick was the first Irish wolfhound with which I had ever had much experience, and I was to have this at close quarters since he would be living in the house with us. Mau Mau terrorists were on the rampage and one of their nastier tricks, in a fairly comprehensive catalogue of unpleasant ideas, was to crucify a dog to it's owner's gate. This put outside kennelling completely out of the question as far as I was concerned, and, in any case, I am a firm believer in having guard dogs close at hand for the times when trouble does occur. I tend to regard them in much the same way as barbed wire entanglements in time of war. They are not there to prevent the enemy getting at you but to hamper him and hold him up long enough to give one the opportunity of doing something about it – like getting your gun out. This business of being quick on the draw is all very well but, when the opposition is coming at you with his weaponry all ready to go, a few seconds respite can be very useful. This made my complement of dogs up to three; I now had Warwick to add to my original Alsatian bitch and ridgeback dog. Quite sufficient to be able to hold up any terrorist intruders long enough for me to empty a couple of barrels of SSG into them.

I knew something of the supposed derivation of the Irish wolfhound and about the bitter controversy which had sur-rounded its entry upon the scene about the middle of the 19th century. In approximately 1840 a Mr Haffield had proclaimed the breed to be extinct and, moreover, that in former days when the wolfhound had existed, it had been very much in the nature of a deerhound. A year or so later a Mr Richardson was saying much the same sort of thing, rather spoiling the effect of his statement by mentioning that he had obtained and was breeding wolfhounds. Perhaps he was trying to make out that the breed was extinct apart from those which he had. He would not be the first and by no means the last discoverer of a rare breed to start putting that sort of message about. However much truth one attaches to the findings of either of these gentlemen, one can probably afford to ignore the accounts of the origin of the breed according to Celtic legend.

This was something to the effect that the giant Finn McCool, had an aunt who was turned into a hound by some sort of Ulster-type

A Russian hunting scene with borzois.

Two borzois in action.

wizard. Finn managed to arrange for the process to be reversed and his aunt once more assumed the form of a woman. All was not, however, quite as perfect as it might have been for whilst she was a hound she had whelped two pups. Although the warlock appeared to have been ready to do all that was in his power to make amends, it seems to have been beyond his capabilities to convert the pups into human beings and, so the story goes, they just had to be content to remain dogs for the rest of their lives. They were named Bran and Sceolaun and were inseparable from Finn McCool, which seems fair enough for, after all, was he not their first cousin? He must have been quite an entertaining sort of person to go around with, being apt to do things like plucking up a handful of earth from the surface of Ulster and flinging it into the Irish Sea, where the proof of the size of his hands still remains in the shape of the Isle of Man, the hole that he left behind being Lough Neagh. For those with the Gaelic I must apologise for my spelling of the name of the hero, which in that tongue would be Fionn mac Cumall.

However an unlikely beginning for the breed this may appear to represent, there are plenty of better authenticated records in early writings in the sagas, but it is a matter of historical fact that Oliver Cromwell prohibited the export of wolfhounds from Ireland, his sound reason being that the decrease in the number of these hounds had been followed by an appreciable increase in the size of the Irish wolf population. Wherever a description of these dogs is found in the old records, it usually seems to mention their being of very light colour and frequently white. This would tend to indicate that these animals were not altogether the same as today's Irish wolfhound.

In 1862 Captain Graham appeared upon the wolfhound scene and he is regarded by some as the restorer of the breed and by others as its inventor. Graham was no dilettante dog fancier; he had previously lived in Ceylon where he had hunted all manner of big game which existed in fair numbers there in those days, employing deerhounds for this purpose. These were the deerhounds of the mid-19th century, very much more of working type than they are today. It is of interest that the bitterest critics of his wolfhounds were the deerhound breeders of that time. Graham recorded his pedigrees meticulously and most of his records survive to this day. According to these it is clear that a very great deal of deerhound blood was used in his breeding programmes. Had his bloodlines been preserved, we would, with little doubt, be in a better position today to make a fairer judgement of his contribution to the breed, but, unfortunately the show fraternity had other ideas. At this distance, it looks very much as though the gallant Captain had painstakingly created, or perhaps recreated, a useful working breed of hound, one which would have proved its value in those days when we were starting to open up all the far-flung corners of the British Empire, so that big game hunting of all kinds not only became available, but also, in many instances, was a necessity.

It was not long, however, before the breed attracted the attention of the dog exhibitors, who, in order to render it the more attractive in their minds, in 1880 introduced great dane blood. Graham's dogs had been between 27 and 32 inches in height, resembling a rather heavily built deerhound, but, in the records which followed the introduction of the exotic blood, the height swiftly shot up to 38 inches. It was the same sorry story of the ruination of working breeds, which by now has extended, with very few exceptions, throughout the breadth of the canine world.

This was where Warwick was an interesting example of the breed for, with a height of 31 inches, small by present day wolfhound standards, and of workmanlike build, he must have resembled those dogs Graham originally bred. Could he have been directly descended from the original strain? Stranger things might have been possible for I never knew much about his background and, like quite a number of the dogs in Kenya, he could have been brought there from South Africa, which was just the sort of place where, in the latter half of the 19th century, they would have been hunting with hounds of the type Graham was breeding. I never heard anything of the Captain hunting there but it is quite likely that he did for a tremendous amount went on between the Cape and places like Ceylon in the days before the opening of the Suez Canal in 1869. What would have been more natural than for a man of Graham's calibre to have given his dogs a try there in the days before the introduction of the great dane blood? If my idea is correct I must have had my mini pack about right for the ridgeback which I had was one of the original Cornelius van Rooyen type, the size of a good big Labrador/retriever, and an excellent hunting dog in every way. This breed was another one which was ruined by the fancy bringing great danes into the breed, and producing the outsized specimens which we see today and which exhibit a good deal more of the dane characteristics than of the ridgeback proper.

On the other hand it is just possible Warwick may have reverted to something resembling the original due to some freakish effect of the combination of altitude and latitude. At the height of over

A wolf hunt.

An Irish wolfhound from earlier this century.

6,000 feet on the Equator some odd things happen to all sorts of organisms, many of which seem to assume a form of development all of their own at the higher altitudes. A good deal is made in travel books concerning the giant lobelias, groundsels and heathers which occur above the forest line in places like Mount Kenya and the Aberdares, but these species are not the only ones which go wild and get a bit out of hand. Another example of something not knowing what its proper size should be being the nettles which one encounters in the forest areas. Not only are these double the size both in length and stoutness of stem of their counterparts in other places, but they also possess a good deal more than double the strength of poison in them, rhinos being about the only form of animal life to be found amongst them. Nor is this discrepancy of size confined to the vegetable kingdom, for where else would one find a pig the size of the giant forest hog – an animal with a shoulder height of 32 inches and an average weight of around two hundredweight? To encounter one of these things in its aboreal habitat is to receive the impression of having walked into a small rhino. They also have a reputation for extreme ferocity when attacked or even when subjected to what they consider to be undue disturbance. African hunters, like the Nderobo who have had a good deal of experience with them, have always told me that these king-sized porkers can never be induced to leave a victim once they have succeeded in getting him down.

It is not simply that some species grow to a larger size than would seem to be strictly normal; others become smaller. One such is the hyrax, a creature not much bigger than a guinea pig which in some ways it rather tends to resemble, its closest living relative, however, being the elephant with which it shares a likeness of physiology. What the things lack in size they more than make up for in noise, making an unearthly din reminiscent of some unfortunate victim having his throat cut with a very blunt knife, this is one of the nastier noises of the African night. So, if any animal is going to revert to type, this would be the place to do it.

On balance, I tend to the opinion that my first hypothesis is more likely to be the correct one for, leaving appearances out of the matter and they are apt to be deceptive, Warwick was a sound and dependable hunting dog which I would scarcely have expected had he been the result of some chance mutation. Not as fast as a deerhound, he was a good stayer and had a good nose on him. It was noticeable that whenever any of my African help were thinking of embarking on a hunting expedition, it was always Warwick that they tried to take with them if they managed to get away with it. I

65

had the dog for only a short period but would dearly have liked him for longer.

As luck would have it, I did manage to retain a part of him for very fortunately my Alsatian bitch, Juno, came in season whilst I was supplying him with board and lodging, and I felt I could not miss this opportunity of a mating. This was duly carried out, and in fact went on for several days, so that at the termination of the nuptials I felt that all had been done that could possibly be done to ensure a fair chance of a litter.

Shortly after this the Colonel turned up and collected Warwick having now completed the construction of his new prison governor's residence in which there was plenty of room for man and dog. Before he departed I informed the Colonel of what had occurred, for Africa is a great place for gossip and I knew that information about the mating would almost certainly be conveyed to him. He seemed delighted about the matter and, I recollect, made some apt remarks as to the duties of lodgers in general and one named Roger in particular.

Juno had her lurcher pups (herding cross longdog) nice and naturally in an old hut just at the back of my house and, as soon as I was able, I brought them all into one of the storerooms which formed part of the rambling ranch house in which we were living. There were eight of them; about half of this number resembled rather rangy Alsatians by the time they had grown out far enough for one to judge, and the rest were light silver grey in colour (yet another throwback to the original wolfhounds which were always spoken of as being light coloured?) and had the appearance of something in the nature of a large and harsh coated saluki. They were to prove themselves to be absolutely perfect for hunting under African bush conditions, although I think they would have been a bit too big for use in this country. Whilst possessing all their sire's stamina, they had a fair bit more speed. As to their IQ, I could not be too sure about this, since under those sort of conditions it was not put to the test in the same way as if I had been hunting them in Britain. I would scarcely have said that they were outstanding in this respect, although, to my mind they possessed a good deal more intelligence than their Alsatian mother, a singularly obtuse animal whose lack of sense has probably quite unjustifiably put me off Alsatians ever since.

From their wolfhound sire they seemed to have inherited a striking degree of staunchness, a quality which I had observed in him during our all too short acquaintance. It was two of these which, together with my trusty old ridgeback Butch, worried a leopard one night. Not a very large leopard, and not without a certain amount of wear and tear on the dogs, but nevertheless an adult leopard, and one that was in no way deficient in either tooth or claw. It was this quality of staunchness, together with good scenting ability and overall stamina, which were of importance to me at the time rather than any great level of intelligence. My breeding a successful litter of hunting dogs was more a matter of good luck than science as in a place like Sirrima, where I was living, 40 or so miles from a town and with one's immediate neighbours a bit sparse on the ground, there was not much choice in any dog breeding programme and one had to make do with whatever was available. In this I was singularly fortunate.

Later on, when I left Sirrima, I took two of the dogs of this breeding with me up to Karamoja in northern Uganda together with my ridgeback. The rest had been given away to suitable homes but naturally those I kept were the tried and trusty ones. They did very well for me in the wild country around Iriri and Namalu but the lifespans of everything and everyone is quite likely to be brought to a sudden termination in places like that, so by the time I returned to Kenya the only dog I still had was my Rhodesian ridgeback, a survivor if ever there was one. He was a brilliant animal in every way save one; although he never bit a member of my family, other people, sometimes including quite close friends, were apt to get a nip from time to time. This made him a bit unpopular. Why he did it remained a bit of a mystery, perhaps ridgebacks just want to reinforce their sense of smell with that of taste from time to time. Another ridgeback I had later on in England displayed similar traits, going for exactly the same part of the anatomy as the first one – in scientific parlance, the lower outer quadrant of the buttock.

Soon after we returned to the United Kingdom I was to become acquainted with yet another Irish wolfhound, but this, unlike Warwick, was the full-sized article, some 36 inches in height. His name was Shonks and he was the property of that highly respected Master of Foxhounds, Captain Charles Barclay. Shortly after returning to these shores I lived for a time (far too short a time) in the delightful north Hertfordshire village of Brent Pelham. It is a place of which I cannot speak too highly, for it seemed to possess every attribute an English village should have, mainly brought about by the positive and unstinting efforts of the Barclays who were everything that members of the squirearchy should be, using the term in its best possible sense. Were there more people like this about, the various societies which exist for the preservation of this and that about the countryside, would largely be redundant.

Shonks turned up as a stray, literally upon the doorstep of Brent Pelham Hall. Everyone went through the usual routine of reporting his presence to the police and so on, but no one came forward to claim him and he became yet another animal on the Barclay strength. It was therefore considered befitting that he should be given a name and this was when he came to be known as Shonks, being called after the local hero of the Pelhams, one Piers Shonks, a somewhat unusual sort of hunting man, unusual in the sort of quarry which he hunted.

The tomb of the original Shonks is in the north wall of Brent Pelham Church where his body has been since soon after the Norman Conquest. He is laid to rest lengthways in the wall, and legend has it that he was placed in this position in order to thwart the intention of the Devil who had vowed that, on Shonks's death, he would take him whether he was interred within the church or outside it. By some sort of ecclesiastical reasoning the conclusion was reached that so long as they placed Shonks's corpse in the wall, it would be neither in nor out of the building and the plans of His Satanic Majesty would be foiled. It seems to have been a fairly devious way of going about it, but one must remember that in those days they were arguing about how many angels could stand on the point of a pin and heretics were being put to the stake for venturing to hold an opinion that Christ had actually smiled. So perhaps in that sort of context it may have made more sense than it seems to today.

Shonks's offence against the Powers of Darkness was that on not one but two occasions he had slain the Devil's creatures, in this case two dragons, one at Brent Pelham and the other in the neighbouring parish of Barkway, and it is said that in his dragon slaying activities Shonks was assisted by a hound of enormous stature. Of course people, hearing the story for the first time, are apt to scoff at it as being mediaeval folk rubbish. But this is not all. Shonks was said to have been a man of considerably more than average size with very long legs, hence his name – Shonks, or Shanks, and when, like so many other ancient churches, Brent Pelham had to go through the usual Victorian restoration, it is on record that during the course of the work the tomb was opened and found to contain the skeleton of a very large man, approaching seven feet in height. This part of the story was thus proven to be correct.

One other fact provides even further food for thought and this is that in the old parish records a rent charge is payable from the

A painting of a wolfhound and its quarry.

parish of Barkway to the parish of Brent Pelham; it dates from the approximate time of Shonks's legendary feat. No one is able to give any reason for the payment of the charge, which may well represent some sort of dragon slaying fee. There are plenty of tales dating from ancient times which have been given a very great deal of credence by both clergy and laity, depite the absence of any proof; one only has to look into the Old Testament in order to find them. I choose to believe the story, more or less in its entirety, and I feel that Piers Shonks should be adopted as the patron saint of pest exterminators. I'll bet the conservationists did not like him much, finishing off the last two dragons in Hertfordshire.

I frequently ponder upon this tale and toy with various notions as to what these creatures, in fact, were which he killed. It has been suggested that they may have been particularly large and ferocious wild boars, but, if this was the case, there existed a perfectly good word in both Norman and Saxon tongues to call them by. So why was it not used? A great many of us are quite confident that there is at least one monster in Loch Ness, as well as others in Loch Morar, and fishermen in the northern waters of the Pentland Firth are said to have seen some fairly inexplicable things at times. Could these have been some sort of survivors from some previous age? It is fairly easy to see how the Devil was brought into the matter, for He was very real in the middle ages; the Church saw to that.

So what better name could have been given to a wolfhound, which turned up unannounced upon the Barclay doorstep? Shortly after this took place, yet another stray dog appeared, a deerhound this time, a bit smaller than Shonks but not much. He also was taken on the strength and appropriately given the name of Dragon. It seems strange that two large dogs of this kind should turn up in the same place at roughly the same time. Coincidence or what? The Pelhams, Brent, Stocking and Furneaux form just the right sort of setting for strange events to occur, lying as they do on an ancient route from London to the North, one which 20 or 30 years ago was still a favourite highway for Romanies, tinkers and persons of that kind. At the time it was also reputed to be a good way of leaving the metropolis without drawing too much attention to oneself.

As far as one was able to discern, Shonks and Dragon were allowed almost total freedom and did not take long to establish themselves as something of local menaces. I do not know whether it was on account of the overwhelming personalities of these two dogs, or whether it indicated the general attitude of the people in the Puckeridge country, but never a soul seemed to take any exception to the escapades of these animals, rather tending to eulogise their misdoings. They were both arrant thieves and stole not only food from kitchens but also articles of clothing from washing lines. When the subject of their villainous activites happened to be of the edible variety, they usually contrived to take away the lot, container and all, in much the same way as my own longdog does. The edibles were, of course, consumed in some secluded spot but the various pots and pans almost always found their several ways to Brent Pelham Hall, from where, having been thoroughly washed and scoured, they were taken by Mrs Barclay to the village shop, to await collection by their rightful owners.

Whilst I was in the village, Shonks's most notorious exploit was to remove a dish of rice pudding from inside an oven. How he did it, no one was able to tell, but did it he did and duly delivered the empty pot back home as proof of his guilt. The only depradation which I ever suffered at his hands, or rather jaws, was to have a leg of lamb removed from by car whilst I was in the act of opening my gate. Alas for Shonks, it was deeply frozen and so he abandoned it by the roadside with two deep tooth marks in it by way of signature. My wife had a close encounter with him one winter evening when she was walking along the narrow unlit lane which led to our house. Part of her way took her by the churchyard and she was somewhat nonplussed to hear the sounds of heavy breathing emanating from the far side of the graveyard wall. Not a vampire, nor a werewolf, although it did tend to resemble the latter to some extent, but Shonks again. Reincarnation or canine race memory? One wonders.

The pair of them, Shonks and Dragon, discovered yet another, to their minds, jolly game. This was to lurk at the bottom of the steep hill, where the road leaves the village in the Bishop's Stortford direction, and pursue cars that laboured up the incline, not tiresomely snapping at the wheels as collies in the back blocks of Ireland will do, but gazing steadfastly through the rear window. This was in the early days of the Mini, when they were priced new at less than £500. There were quite a number of these little cars about at the time and I had it on very good authority, first hand in fact, that a good deal of consternation was caused by motorists looking into their rear view mirrors and observing four legs of some shaggy beast directly to the rear of the vehicle. The mischievious creatures managed to keep up with most cars that went up this particular hill, which demonstrated that they had not only a fair turn of speed but also a good staying capacity. This, coupled with their prowess at retrieving all those baking dishes and other kitchen utensils and carrying them back home, seems to indicate that either of these dogs, given a certain amount of the right sort of training, would have become a useful hunting dog, particularly if provided with the right sort of quarry to engage.

With Shonks and, as an earlier example, Warwick, as my yardsticks of the Irish wolfhound, I would not hesitate to use the right type of this breed of dog in pursuit of any large game. In fact the capabilities of Warwick and the dogs which I bred from him were proven to my full satisfaction in this respect. Whilst I have never had the privilege of hunting wolf, I have taken hyena with my wolfhound hybrids and these creatures are reputed to possess the most powerful jaws of any of the carnivores, including lion and tiger. They never showed themselves to be backward on leopard either. But I would not consider the present day wolfhound to be suitable for hunting the various quarry to be found in the British Isles.

The Borzoi

Although its development followed a very different path, the borzoi is a wolfhound, a Russian wolfhound, in fact. In general appearance they differ from the Irish wolfhound a good deal and appear to have altogether more of the longdog about them. At first sight it might appear that these exceedingly elegant animals may have a considerable degree of application as a working dog, until one comes to consider the almost over developed long thin skull of the beast. But is this a very good way of assessing a dog's IQ? A good deal is made of the dolichocephalic skull as it is called by the denigrators of longdogs, most of whom are avid supporters of the invincibility of the collie blooded lurcher. When seeking to draw conclusions from physical appearance, it might be as well to bear in mind that the enormous jaws of the longdog, jaws specifically engineered by nature for the purpose of laying hold of prey add to this impression of a long thin head. Given a shorter and broader jaw, the heads of most breeds of longdog would not give quite such an impression of Algie, the chinless wonder.

Having put that point I must say that, in my experience the borzois I have encountered have never conveyed any very great impression of being over bright, but this, I feel, is much more likely to be connected with the task for which they were bred, rather than anything to do with the shape of their heads. One has to be very careful about judging a book by its cover for it is a comparatively easy matter to take such ideas a step or two further and wind up amongst the dangerous theories put forward by the Nazis concerning different races. It is ludicrous to believe that a person with a long thin head is inferior in any way to one with a short wide one, so why apply such imaginings to the IQ of dogs?

A Russian huntsman with a brace of borzois.

To consider the purpose for which these dogs were evolved one must realise that they were bred and worked with a specific quarry in mind, namely the wolf, the coursing of which was the subject of stringent convention, making it even more of a formal proceeding than coursing hares under rules in this country. The quarry first of all had to be located, and this part of the proceedings was carried out by officials who were in the nature of gamekeepers. Having located the wolf, it was driven from cover by a pack of hounds which were not unlike our own foxhounds in appearance and in the way they worked. Their task, however, consisted only of putting the wolf out of cover and, as soon as that was accomplished, their job was done. They were in no way required to kill the beast or even attack it. I dare say that this must have sometimes occurred and must have amounted to a faux pas of the dimensions of shooting a fox in the Shires. There were occasions, of course, and locations when and where a wolf was not to be found. When this happened a wolf was conveyed to the scene of the activities in an iron cage. In such cases there was no disguising the fact as would have been the case with a bagged fox in this country and, in fact, the caged beast was sometimes paraded before the hunt.

Borzois from the Woronzova hunt.

Having been put out of cover by the hounds, or alternatively let out of its cage, on to a predetermined coursing ground, a pair of borzois were slipped on to the wolf. Like the hounds in the first place, the task of the borzois was also of a somewhat formal nature, for they were trained not to kill the wolf, but to tip it over and pin it, until such time as their owner arrived, dismounted from his horse and despatched the wolf with the short sword with which he was armed. Sometimes a leash of three dogs was slipped, in which case the work required of them was exactly the same as where a pair was employed. On occasion, presumably when the quarry was a bit thin on the ground, the wolf was taken alive, caged and removed from the scene, to be carted away to be chased another day, much in the same manner as carted deer, and at other times to be used for the training of the young entry of borzois. Taking a wolf alive sounds like something of a feat, although probably once anyone gets the knack of it, it would present no more difficulties, if as many, as are experienced in the capture of any large carnivore alive. I should think that the biggest risk that was run in handling these animals was that of contracting rabies from them. There was a great deal of rabies about in Russia in those days and a wolf which was going through the quiescent stage of this disease would appear, at first sight, quite a suitable subject for live catching.

I understand that coursing meetings between borzois are sometimes held, not at wolves, of course, caged or otherwise, but at hares. To date I have not witnessed one of these events, but those of my acquaintances who have do not seem to have been favourably impressed with the performance. There are two borzois that I see about which are the property of a Russian lady, one is not in the slightest way interested in pursuing anything and the other will go after rabbits, but, on catching up with them, will run round and round them making no attempt to pick up.

Another acquaintance of mine who runs a boarding kennel and also does a bit of dog dealing (on the basis of all successful trading – if you can acquire your merchandise for nothing, you can scarcely fail to show a profit on selling it) was given a borzoi bitch. He had a certain amount of difficulty in finding anyone to buy it, thus tending to confound the theory of profitable dealing and had her in his establishment long enough for us to run her at a hare on a few occasions. The result was so similar each time as to become predictable. On each run she displayed no interest whatsoever in the hare, but turned her attentions upon the other dog, endeavouring to catch it with the obvious intention of killing it and, I am quite sure she would have succeeded in carrying out her purpose had we not been pretty quick off the mark ourselves. On this showing, perhaps they might be of some use as a specialist fox killer, but with other more handy dogs available, who would go to the length of using one?

—6—

The Whippet

MY PERSONAL EXPERIENCE with longdogs commenced nearly 60 years ago when I was away at school.
Which meant my being away from home, and moreover
being away from my terriers, ferrets and .410, for periods of some
three months at a stretch. There was no remission for good
behaviour or half-term break and a three month term was a three
month term. No doubt there were other establishments of this
nature, where perhaps a rather more enlightened attitude towards
the pupils prevailed, just as there must have been schools where the
disciplinary process was even more rigorous – Dotheboys Hall for
instance.

On the whole, whilst in no way holding any sort of opinion that
one's schooldays are the best days of one's life (a smug belief which
seemed to be all too readily forthcoming from the lips of just about
every adult one came into contact with), I looked upon my being
there as some sort of necessary evil which, if not capable of being
cured, must simply be endured. Always having been one who
sought to make the best of his situation whatever this has happened
to be, I strove not to endure anything more than was strictly
necessary. The academic side of life did not bother me to any
extent – being blessed with a good memory I discovered that by
keeping my mouth shut and my ears open I could scrape by very
nicely with what I heard in class, supplemented by the two and a
half hours prep we endured each evening.

The one aspect of school life I was unable to perceive any value in whatsoever and whole heartedly loathed, was that of compulsory games. These occupied what was, to my mind, an inordinate amount of one's non-academic time and it was not long before I hit upon a means of avoiding them, or at any rate, some of them. This was quite simply accomplished by pretending to develop some kind of ailment, in my own case usually a simulated head cold. When supposedly suffering in this respect, I learned that instead of taking part in organised games, one was required to take the Headmaster's wife's dog for a walk. When I discovered this to be a small white-bodied terrier which had been obtained from the kennels of the South Wold Hunt, I swiftly made it my business to become an even more successful malingerer, to such effect that after a year or two of this there were suspicions that I might be suffering from some form of chronic illness. This was at about the same time that I contracted ringworm, picked up from the very unhygenic calf pens in a tumbledown farmyard I used to frequent in search of rats. At any rate, I was considered to be 'delicate'; a few years later I was passed as A1 plus for the paratroops.

Meanwhile the terrier, which until then had not been encouraged to participate in any form of hunting, began to come to life and became quite useful as soon as I entered it to rabbit. Its capabilities became even more abundantly obvious when of its own accord it entered to fox. Although it gave me a few anxious moments, it was good at avoiding trouble and the earths were not deep. It swiftly became adept at getting in and out of these unmarked, frequently bolting a fox in the process.

It was not long before a further bonanza came my way, this time in the shape of a largish whippet, the property of the school handyman. He (the handyman) was an all round fieldsportsman of the artisan hunter type, and, as so frequently occurs, common interests soon gave rise to common confidences. By this time someone had noticed that the terrier had developed a strong partiality for the chase and so, whenever I took it out, I was given strict instructions not to let it off the lead. Out of sight, out of mind, however, was the order of the day at that age and I paid scant attention to these prohibitions. The effect of this was that the creature became so keen a hunter that it was eventually returned from whence it had come – the hunt kennels – where, no doubt, it lived a much happier, fuller and altogether more useful existence. Its replacement was an old and steady spaniel the exercising of which I did not seem to be entrusted with. This suited me very well since the whippet was coming along very nicely.

In those days, long before the vile myxomatosis had been introduced, the sheer quantity of rabbits on the sand land farms, many of which were semi-derelict with their occupiers eking out some sort of precarious existence on a wing and a prayer, had to be seen to be believed. Indeed on many of these miserable holdings, where the main agricultural enterprise seemed to consist of growing a few acres of rye and rearing a few skinny sheep and an emaciated cow or two, the main source of revenue must have been from rabbits, even at sixpence a couple, which was the price they made when the market bottomed out at harvest-time. The gin trap had not yet been declared illegal and provided a fairly simple way of making large catches, but any means that happened to be available was used to deal with the long-eared pests including shooting as many as possible when the corn was being harvested and, after that, snaring, trapping and until they started to breed, ferreting those that were left.

Harvest came along during the summer holidays and I was strongly encouraged to be in the cornfield whenever the binder was cutting the crop, my .410 at the ready. The headkeeper's house was situated more or less in the centre of the larger of the two farms which my father rented from Sir Berkeley Sheffield, and so it would have been unusual for him not to be present at such times. My education in this respect was therefore not neglected for things had to be done in precisely the correct way. No dogs were allowed in the field, the chasing of rabbits with sticks was frowned upon, and by the time the binder was getting towards the end of the field, there usually seemed to be someone at each corner of the standing corn, gun in hand. Woe betide anyone who shot a sitting rabbit or a black one, (these having been put down by the keepers and used as an indication of whether there was any poaching going on). People tended to behave themselves properly on these occasions for headkeepers, like huntsmen, have a forceful turn of phrase and Matt Grass was no exception.

One occasion comes to mind when the son of our landlord, back from Eton for the vacation, happened to discharge his gun at one of the black rabbits with lethal result. 'You've shot the bloody parson, you dozy little sod!' roared Grass at the son of his employer. He had no respect for anyone when it came to preserving game and I thought, at times, that he must know each one of the black rabbits individually. His other strictures were also not without sound foundation – a dog in a harvest field could easily get after a rabbit or hare and wind up in the knives of the binder, which in those horse-powered days was not easy to stop suddenly; likewise, people tearing around in pursuit of fleeing bunnies, something which seemed to result in a state of near hysteria although no doubt, a highly exciting interlude in otherwise boring lives, was not only an unmitigated nuisance, getting in the way of everyone in general, but also presenting a highly unedifying spectacle reminiscent of what must have gone on in the days of bull baiting.

An excellent all round hunting whippet.

Even before the stooked corn was carried from the fields, snares were being set in all the likely places, although with the higher proportion of grassland in those days, one had to make sure they were not put down in any pastures where stock might be grazing. I have known of more than one bullock with its tongue torn out due to a thoughtlessly set snare. As soon as the take from snares began to fall off, the gin traps went into the entrances of the rabbit burrows. These were highly efficient and almost anyone could set them so as to catch rabbits, but again they could prove to be something of a menace to livestock, particularly dogs, and three-legged canines were not all that uncommon in country districts. A heavy toll of poaching cats was also exacted whenever traps went down close to human habitation and many an old maiden lady's pet tomcat ended his days in a rabbit trap.

By the time the undergrowth was down and ferreting could be started, I was back at school, wondering whether by the following Saturday afternoon I might be able to feign some maladie imaginaire, say some slight infection of the respiratory system, serious enough for me to be excused games but sufficiently trivial to keep me out of the sick room. Having pulled that one off successfully, the next item on the agenda was to ensure that Syd's whippet was available. It usually was.

Thus it came about that I made my first acquaintance with a longdog, ironically something that could never have occurred had I remained at home as a day boy at a local school. Not only was my father a tenant on an estate where the preservation of game was put above all other considerations, but we were in the midst of other large estates where similar ideas prevailed. It was not until one reached Lord Yarborough's Brocklesby Estate that a somewhat more enlightened outlook prevailed. Just as long as his Lordship's tenants took care to preserve a few foxes, pretty near anything else was overlooked and keeping the odd whippet or lurcher was in no way denigrated.

The whippet of which I write was a brindle bitch, about four years of age and standing about 20 inches at the shoulder. If anyone were to say that she had a touch of greyhound blood, I would certainly not argue the point. Most of the whippets one encountered in the Lincolnshire countryside of those days would now be reckoned a bit on the large side and some of them were quite definitely a trifle coarse in the coat. None of those with which I became acquainted possessed anything in the form of pedigree, other than by word of mouth going back a generation or two. They were as hard as flint and eager to hunt, at the same time being sufficiently biddable for a kid, such as myself aged 12 or so, to take out and run on his own.

This was the time of derelict farms and holdings run on a principle of low farming – dog and stick places. Places of this sort paid little, if any rent and the landowners had to make corresponding economies. Estate workers were amongst the first to feel the crunch and fairly early on in the process of running down, the services of gamekeepers were relinquished. The place where my father farmed was owned by a wealthy man in his own right who did not have to rely upon the tenant farmers for his main income. Being a decent sort of chap, he was always ready to overlook the matter of rent in the case of anyone who was having a rough time of it, just so long as they respected his game and were the subject of satisfactory reports from his headkeeper. My luck in having access to a partly derelict countryside with no gamekeepers, friendly though penniless farmers and a first rate whippet was something in the nature of hitting the jackpot. The friendly farmers soon became even more friendly when they discovered I was capable of killing off a good many of their rabbits – rabbits which they full well knew I was quite unable to take away for I had nowhere to take and sell them.

The main privation I considered myself to be labouring under at that time was being unable to get out after dark and I felt I was missing out in not being able to take part in the various netting operations which Syd and his brother were wont to undertake whenever the night was right. I heard all about them all right, and also about the lamping which was done. Not lamping as we know it today with a dog running down the beam, but a totally different way of doing things, in which the dog went over the stubbles with a small lamp attached to its collar, the object of its activities being to drive the game into the net. In those days stubbles were frequently not ploughed, particularly in the areas of lower farming, until after Christmas and so there was a fair amount of running ground open to anyone who happened to be that way inclined. It was quite surprising what managed to find its way into the net, rabbits being far from the only consideration. With the right sort of dog, which could be relied upon to keep things on the move at a nice, steady rate, the haul of pheasants and partridges could be quite phenomenal. I did not indulge in this sort of hunting myself, but the best take of pheasants that I ever saw was 37 brace in one drive. I gathered that this was not at all out of the way and that far larger bags were quite commonplace.

Of the type of lamping which is done these days about the only example that we ever saw was in rat catching around stackyards. It seems quite incredible today how circumstances can have altered over the space of a mere 50 or so years, although things must have seemed just as revolutionary in the latter half of the 19th century when, first of all there appeared the threshing machine, shortly followed by the sail reaper, which lasted only a decade or so before being superseded by the reaper binder. For centuries before this it had been scythes and hand tied sheaves, which were put into stook for what was considered to be the requisite length of time – barley only having to hear the church bells once, wheat twice and oats three times. After this minimum period, always depending upon the weather, the corn could be stacked in the right sort of way with the narrower steading for barley, which it was exceedingly important should in no way become over-heated with consequent loss of its malting qualities.

Later in life I had the good fortune to spend some years amongst people who thought a scythe a highly sophisticated piece of equipment. People who, when instructed to off-load a lorry full of sacks of maize, and being provided with a wheelbarrow to lighten their labours, had put a sackful or two of maize into the barrow and then carried the whole lot, sacks, wheelbarrow, the lot, to the store never having been introduced to the wheel before. I suppose that in line with today's mealy mouthed and patronising outlook, I should be saying that it made me feel ever so humble to have witnessed this sort of proceeding, but in point of fact it did nothing of the sort. I forthwith taught them, amongst other things, what a wheel was about so that, a couple of years later, several of their number were driving tractors, whilst they, in their turn, showed me what real hunting was about. For the record, they learned all about wheels a good deal faster than I grasped the rudimentary elements of tracking, but I still entertained no feelings of being ever so humble – this is for the Uriah Heaps amongst us, many of whom manage to make a fat living out of their hypocrytic self-abasement.

To get back to the stackyard; this was the nerve-centre of the farm. This was the place to which the crops were carried and it was

A fine looking coursing whippet.

A picture of keeness.

on its outskirts that the horse stables, cow shed, pig styes and so on were situated so that the sustenance for the animals might be readily available. The farmer's house, or that of his bailiff if the place were sufficiently large to warrant one, or a hind if it did not, was usually located somewhere not far away, sometimes being so close as to be semi-detached with a cow or horse stable. This arrangement may seem a bit unhygenic in today's circumstances but had a very great deal to recommend it, when electric power and mechanical transport were not readily available. A perfect arrangement in many ways, apart from one small item – the presence of rattus norvegicus, the brown rat. The corn stacks provided perfect homes for these creatures, the sort of accommodation that we have all been after at some time in our lives, with plenty of insulation against winter chills and summer heats, a safe haven against our enemies (well comparitively safe anyway) and an abundant, never failing supply of food located close at hand. From a rodent point of view, however, there was a snag, if indeed they possess a point of view. (I am a bit doubtful whether or not they have, for they are singularly intelligent creatures.) This was that once a year their house, their home, their entire environment was demolished and flung into the ever hungry mouth of the threshing machine. This was the moment when being a rat was perhaps not quite such a good idea, and the time when terriers and their kin proved their worth.

Many of the farmers in my own part of the country had a somewhat ambivalent attitude towards threshing the harvested crop. For one thing, the corn harvest was swiftly followed by the lifting of potatoes, these in their turn being followed by sugar beet and other root crops, and this occupied most of the available time up to Christmas. It was in the early part of the New Year, when frequently the fields were covered with snow or frozen iron hard so that field work was brought to a standstill, that most of the corn was threshed. By then ample time had been provided for rats and mice to come in from the fields in order to take up their winter quarters. This was the time that yet another form of lamping took place. Most nights one or two of us would go into the stackyard with a paraffin hurricane lamp and a terrier or two. In those days long pointed rods of iron, up to eight or nine feet in length were used during the summer and autumn when the hay and barley was being stacked. These were thrust into the heart of the stacks and left there for the first few weeks. They were withdrawn daily in order to test the temperature of the ricks, which were in the habit of heating up to the point of spontaneous combustion had the crop been carted with a bit too much moisture in it. Should they become overheated, the laborious task of turning them over had to be carried out, and the rest of the local rustic population, ever pleased to see a neighbour in trouble, would slyly look at one another, saying: 'I see old so-and-so has lost his watch.'

Apart from this, their more valuable function was when we lads shoved them into the corn ricks wherever we discerned any rodent activity. A direct hit with one of the needle sharp points could be relied upon to shift any hapless rat from its cosy nest and send it bolting out into the jaws of the waiting terrier. Or so one hoped, for the lights were dim and projected their feeble rays for no more than a few feet, so the quarry frequently managed to effect its escape. The usual route for exit was by way of the iron and along the arm of whoever was pushing it in, a quick rush past his ear and a nosedive from his shoulder. We had never heard of leptospirosis and the like and so were little worried by the proximity of the beasts. When threshing took place, the exodus of rats was often quite spectacular, or at least appeared to be so at the time.

It was on one such occasion that I had my first experience of a whippet dealing with rats. With Syd's whippet bitch at heel, I chanced a visit to a farm not a million miles from the village of North Willingham, a place where I could usually borrow a ferret or two to indulge in a spot of hedgerow rabbiting. As I arrived at the farm that Wednesday afternoon in February it was evident that the threshing of a stack of wheat was well forward. The stack was one I was already familiar with for had I not been getting the odd rat from it whenever I had had the opportunity to stick a ferret into it? 'Blame'. Thoo should 'ave been 'ere airf an 'oor ago,' exclaimed the friendly farmer by way of greeting me, like the rest of his kind ready to give credit where it was due. 'Iver so many 'as gotten away, so shape theesen and get wot's left. . . . If any's left,' he added darkly.

Assuming that he referred to the rats that had been in the stack and knowing my Lincolnshire farming population pretty well by this time, I formed the opinion that two or, at a pinch, perhaps three, had escaped, so I took up a position with the bitch between the remains of the corn stack and a sluggish watercourse which ran some 20 or 30 feet away. I reckoned it would take about half an hour to finish the stack off for there were only some two or three courses of sheaves left above the bean straw steadling. Nothing much happened until the steadle was reached and then the rats erupted. Only the one bitch was present but she, aided and abetted by a few of us with handy sticks and our hob nailed boots, managed to put paid to over 20 rats. It was the first time I had witnessed a whippet in action in these sort of circumstances and I feel that I can justifiably say that she proved to be a better rat killer than many of the terriers I have encountered both before and since.

Since those days I have had a good deal to do with whippets and at present I frequently work with two excellent specimens of the breed. In a one man, one dog relationship I would consider them

Two racing dogs showing the versatility of the whippet.

hard to beat for rabbiting and occasional ratting, since a good whippet will fill the roles of both terrier and running dog. They are not bad on hares either, providing the hare is not given too much law, but I would judge them to be a bit light for fox although should one learn the knack, their jaws have sufficient power to deal with the situation. They possess plenty of other plus factors as well. With their short, smooth coats, they are no trouble to keep clean and are easily dried off whenever they get wet. Being of handy size and not usually much exceeding 20 or so pounds in weight, they are easily picked up and transported, as well as fitting comfortably beneath the seats of most of the pubs I use. I do not want to make too much of this benefit but in some of the establishments I frequent, more fights seem to be provoked by lurchers being trodden on than for any other reason. Whippets were kept more in mining communities than anywhere else in times gone by, and such characteristics as curling up out of the way and keeping clean seem to have been bred into them.

Although this is a book about longdogs and not lurchers it is difficult to write about the modern whippet without talking about the whippet/Bedlington cross. One sees a good many small lurchers about these days. These attractive little beasts are deservedly popular but I sometimes wonder if they really possess any real advantage over the pure bred whippet. It is very true that the first crosses of this breeding remain on the whole remarkably true to type and in conformation, resemble a sort of mini-deerhound, but, should the breeding programme be extended, some funny looking results can and do appear. I think that the reason so many people go for this cross may be that they are under the impression that pure bred whippets, having a smooth coat, must tend to be greatly affected by the cold. This, indeed, seems to be a quite widely held opinion judging by some of the outsize whippet coats which are sometimes seen in wintertime. Some of the hairier coats alter the general appearance of the wearer to something resembling those diminutive donkeys, almost invisible under enormous loads of brushwood, which one used to see around the Eastern Mediterranean regions. I have never found the whippets I have known to suffer from the cold to any marked extent and I have been out hunting with them in temperatures well below zero without noticing any visible signs of distress. Just so long as they are adequately housed and bedded, I would not expect them to differ much from any other sort of smooth coated dog in this respect.

Two whippets in full flight after a hare.

These days there must be whippet owners who wish to use their dogs for lamping. For this sort of work, they would prove to be completely adequate, just so long as things are kept within some sort of reasonable limits. In other words, if you are content to go out for an hour or so and run a few rabbits, all well and good, but a good many dogs, mainly lurchers with a lot of stamina, have been ruined and in some cases run to death at this job. So just know when enough is enough and be prepared to leave it at that. Some of the extravagant claims which are made by a certain type of lurcher owner and which some of the sporting periodicals are weak

Slipping two whippets.

minded enough to publish, do nothing but harm in this respect. Circumstances can differ enormously between various parts of the country and where, in some places, it would present no great problem to take comparitively large numbers of rabbits, there are others where it would be a bit of a strain to bag half a dozen.

Some of these tales of huge kills remind one of the tasteless shooting exploits of people like Payne-Gallway. These sort of accounts of slaughter tend to remind one of the Somme and Ypres, and should never in any way be confused with the quite different records of those who have killed either for the pot or to control something that has become a pest.

To get back to lamping, however, there is no great sporting merit in this either; all sorts of dogs, including a good many sheepdogs are very good at it. As a way of cutting down the numbers of rabbits when they have become a nuisance or to catch a couple or so rabbits for a pie, it is excellent. But as sport I do not rate lamping very high and, as a way of boasting how many rabbits a dog has taken, not at all.

One important aspect of the Bedlington/whippet cross concerns the sort of Bedlington with which one crosses one's whippet.

Whereas it is easy enough to find a whippet that would do the job, the Bedlington side of the equation can present the breeder with a certain amount of problems, always assuming that he is an honest breeder and not merely trying to breed some Bedlington/whippet pups for the sole reason that he thinks they will produce a quick profit. Just as anyone might wonder what exactly a lurcher or a longdog might be, in the same way it has come to the stage of wondering what a Bedlington might be. By the same token one might wonder what any of the breeds registered with the Kennel Club might be, but it is only in the case of working dogs that this might matter. As with some other breeds, strange things have been happening to Bedlingtons over the last few decades with Cruft's-crazed exhibitors striving for ever fancier looking coats and even more accentuated roach backs. All well and good in the times when they were introducing a bit of whippet blood for this could only have led to a more sporting type of dog but, looking at today's show bench Bedlingtons, one just begins to wonder whether something smaller like an Italian greyhound may not have been brought in resulting in a smaller, lighter boned animal than it should be.

Worse still, there appears to be little doubt that poodle blood has been brought in and miniature poodle at that. Nowadays, we seem to have lost sight of the fact that quite so many of these highly popular miniature breeds were developed by the simple expedient of inbreeding the smallest dogs – the runts – in each litter. I think it unlikely that anyone would bring in poodle blood in order to improve the working capabilities of any sort of terrier and therefore need scarcely say more on this particular point other than to suggest that anyone keen to breed the whippet/Bedlington hybrid, other than those bitten by the small lurcher showing bug, should be careful about the source he obtains the Bedlington side of the mixture from. It is essential that the blood is of a working strain, the best of which comes from the incomparable dogs of George Newcombe's Rillington strain and the late Mrs Williamson's Gutchcommon strain.

At the same time it may be well to remember that whilst the working Bedlington in many ways resemble in appearance and performance the Bedlingtons of old, this has, in many cases, been brought about and subsequently maintained by the recent introduction of other terrier blood. Any efforts to extend one's particular line of Bedlington/whippet hybrids beyond the first cross may lead to the appearance of unexpected and unwanted characteristics inherited from a relative of completely different terrier type to the Bedlington. It would also be worth remembering that the whippet you are breeding from could also have a terrier ancestor not very far back. As anyone with even a rudimentary knowledge of genetics will realise a Bedlington/whippet litter could produce some totally unexpected results. Therefore the most rigorous culling of litters is of vital importance. This is an aspect of breeding too often neglected in any case, but one which becomes even more necessary in such circumstances as this.

Taking a breather before the final at the East of England Whippet Coursing Club meeting at Duxford.

Although today the Bedlington terrier is the breed which is most frequently crossed with the whippet – the most favoured arrangement being ¾ whippet to ¼ Bedlington – this has not always been the case. A very popular cross some 40 or 50 years ago was with an Irish terrier. The result was a remarkably neat looking little hound with a useful broken coat, which was just sufficient to afford a good degree of resistance to the elements without being long enough to be a nuisance. They were very useful little rabbiting and vermin dogs but the ones which came my way seemed a bit inadequate for taking on a hare. I do not recollect ever seeing the cross of an Irish terrier on to a greyhound but no doubt they were about and I would have expected them to be capable of taking on just about anything, for the Irish terrier of those days, prior to its becoming yet another casualty of the show bench, was a formidable sort of creature in its own right. Matt Grass always said that the best ratting dog he had ever encountered was an Irish terrier. This had been in the days when he had been a keeper on the Duke of Westminster's Estate at Eaton in Cheshire and so must have been in the early years of this century. The animal was much in demand at threshing time when its party piece was to consume the first three or four rats it caught, after that being content to give each of them a powerful nip and get on with the next one – the mark of any good ratter. It is a dreadful shame that all these good old working breeds of terrier have gone, for apart from being useful dogs to any sort of vermin, they also provided useful crossing material in the production of lurchers.

A perfect slip.

Another point that should be stressed is the advisability of obtaining one's stock from a reliable source – somewhere where the dogs are bred for work. Just about any sort of whippet will catch rabbits but when one sees the way a dog of the right sort goes about the job it leaves very little doubt as to the type at which one should be aiming. The whippet coat does seem to vary a bit and I would tend to avoid the silkier coated varieties, although I must say that I have seen many of these fine coated little beauties getting amongst all sorts of thorny scrub in order to get on closer terms with their quarry and being none the worse for it.

The best whippets I have encountered to date are bred in Hertfordshire. These are bred for coursing and I would recommend acquiring one from a coursing rather than a show or racing background if you want a working dog. A dog acquired from this breeding some years back I consider to be one of the best rabbiting dogs I have ever encountered. With all due respects to both the dog and its owner, I would not go so far as to say that it is an example of canine beauty, most whippets are beautiful little creatures, but there has to be an exception to every rule. But then beauty is as beauty does. If I had to choose my ideal hunting companion from all the dogs I have ever known, this one would be pretty near the top of the list. Although I would by no means expect him to take all before him at Cruft's, should any sporting man need just one dog to fill just about every function required of him, the whippet is the one to choose.

There is but one snag, however, with whippets from a working strain and, the better the hunter the worse the fault as a rule. They do frequently tend to remind one that they have terrier in their origins when they lay hold of their prey. So should you be one of those fussy people who object to the sight of an occasional mangled and very dead rabbit, perhaps this would not be your sort of dog since they can sometimes be hard mouthed. Since I only hunt for my own stewpot or for the purpose of pest control, this is not a failing that worries me overmuch.

This slightly hard aspect of the breed has one very good, if perhaps overlooked bonus as many whippets are very good guard dogs. Like many other longdogs, when engaged in the chase they remain as quiet as one would obviously wish a dog to be, but as soon as they are entrusted with the task of keeping an eye on your property, their terrier ancestors are not long in coming to the fore and they can become quite noisy if disturbed by prowlers. Should it become necessary, they are quite ready to follow up this hostile demonstration with even more positive action. My grandfather had a whippet at the time he had an outlying farm on the Lincolnshire wolds; still something of an out of the way sort of place today, it was even more so when he was there nearly a century ago. Although crime was in no way the problem it is today, there were still quite a few ugly customers about, particularly since the place where he lived was on one of the more favoured of the vagrants' routes between the workhouses at Horncastle and Market Rasen. Even by the time I was at school, tramps were still using this road, having had a night or so in one spike and being on their way to the next one. There was a well recognised circuit which all of them used to follow and, from what I saw of them, although many were decent enough fellows, quite genuinely making the best that they could of things during some exceedingly hard times, there could not help but be some fairly unpleasant characters amongst their number. It was thus a matter of some importance that isolated farmsteads should be adequately protected and this was a role at which my grandfather's whippet was reputed to excel.

Two whippets running up to a hare.

As is so often the case, however, the time he really gave of his best in this respect was at the expense of a totally innocent party, this time a harmless Italian organ grinder. He, poor soul, decided to give a rendering of those airs which his humble instrument was capable of producing but unfortunately, in more ways than one, he chose a day when the entire household was away at market, the sole occupant and custodian being the whippet, which, until the musician put in his appearance, had been dozing in the stackyard. At the rear of the farmhouse there was a walled courtyard and this was the location the musician chose to render his obligato. As the first strains of the overture to *Aida* were to be heard, the dog took extreme exception to the performance and kept the unfortunate chap penned up in a corner of the yard until my grandparents returned home several hours later.

There are other benefits in owning a whippet. Not only is the show bench open to you but also, as the owner of a registered dog, your local whippet racing track and the coursing meetings organised by various clubs. You will also find that you have a very pleasant and intelligent companion. As I get older I have often thought I would be quite content to end my hunting days as they started, in the company of a whippet.

—7—

Breeding

MOST OF THOSE who hunt with longdogs will probably be of the opinion that the crossbred is a better choice than the purebred. Mind you, should you be solely engaged in rabbiting, then a purebred whippet takes a good deal of beating but, apart from the coursing strains of these excellent little dogs, most people will probably agree that most breeds of longdog are the better for being crossed with some other breed of longdog and the greyhound, in most instances, forms the basis of the cross. There are some who wish to take the matter that bit further and breed three-quarter greyhounds, but where this may be of benefit in lurcher breeding, when breeding longdog to longdog, the half bred gives the best results. Hybrid vigour certainly enters into the matter and, by now, most of us must be aware to some degree of what this means in practical terms.

Hybrid vigour
It is a factor of which I have been aware for quite a long time, starting off by crossing Tamworth pigs with Berkshires to produce things which, in some ways, resembled porcine leopards but which did better and progressed faster than either of the parent breeds. Following these forays into outcrossing, which took place in the 1930s (they would be somewhat more difficult to accomplish these days due to the decline in both breeds to a point where one would

have to go to the Rare Breeds Society to find them) I have continued breeding along these lines more or less ever since, whether it be dogs, cattle in the African bush or bees at the end of my orchard. For an exceedingly amateur geneticist such as myself, the first cross is by far the surest and most rapid route to success, usually turning out to be that little bit better than either of the parents. In my long lost youth I was frequently being advised to breed pure, and make money and earn respect that way. Sound enough advice in its way I suppose should one wish to wind up at Cruft's if one is breeding dogs, or the Royal Agricultural Show if one is involved in the production of other sorts of livestock. Not the life for me, however, preferring as I do a quiet time of it with as little cut throat competition as possible. Hybrid vigour though only

A deerhound/greyhound (L) and a three-quarter deerhound/greyhound (R).

applies to mating one purebred to another, but different, pure-bred. If you cross a borzoi/saluki/deerhound with a whippet/collie/greyhound/saluki you will have created a genetic melting pot which is likely to produce a very high percentage of rubbish. There will be physically and mentally very little uniformity and they certainly will not have 'that little bit extra' that is associated with a cross between two purebreds.

Our native breeds of longdog, the greyhound, the deerhound

and the whippet are far from being deficient in grey matter. Moreover, as well as being fairly bright on the whole, they have, over the centuries, adapted themselves to our local conditions. We have only to cross one of these breeds with the other and we set free all sorts of useful genes, which accounts for the unparalleled examples of hybrid vigour when any of these are interbred.

Uniformity

A famous geneticist called Hagedoorn says on the subject of cross-breeding that all crossbreds usually conform to type within the first cross, irrespective of the characteristics of both parents. As an example he cites a visit he made to the mule sales, to which the mule foals are brought along with their dams. Despite the very mixed sample of mares, Hagedoorn mentions that he noticed a very marked uniformity amongst the foals. This may well be correct; in fact I would accept that this statement must be correct when it has been put on record by a skilled observer of Hagedoorn's standard, but he goes on to quote various examples of poultry, cattle and horses, in which he mentions that he has discovered evidence to corroborate his findings in this respect. My own experience with mules has been of a limited nature and, although I have used them, I have never bred them and so am unable to comment upon this aspect. My own experience in this respect has been mainly with cattle and sheep and dogs where I have been aware that the uniformity of type which Hagedoorn mentions does not always come through. With certain breeds it does tend to occur but with others it certainly does not. I have found that degrees of variance occur within the first generation hybrids amongst many crosses of dogs. On the whole, the Bedlington/whippet crossbred is fairly predictable, as is the grey-hound/deerhound hybrid but this is only on a basis of using first rate specimens as foundation stock. Use second rate parents and you will swiftly discover that the progeny is uniform enough in one respect at least – it is not worth keeping.

Even in those instances where the first generation hybrid exhibits a certain uniformity of type in physical make-up, there can be, and frequently is, a marked disparity in mental ability and this is the best of reasons for ensuring that the parent stock on both sides has the highest canine IQ that it is possible to find. When selecting your bitch and dog to breed from do not just take looks into account but more importantly choose those that show the best physical and mental qualities required in a hunting dog. Make a list of these points that you want in your pup and look for a bitch and a stud dog that possess these, for instance if you take on a hard bitch that has a vicious nature because it is going for free, do not be surprised if this comes through in the pups even if the sire is the best tempered dog imaginable. Also remember that if your ideal height for a longdog is 26" choose two parents who are, as nearly as possible, this height – do not imagine that if you breed a whippet to a 30" greyhound they will oblige and split the difference in height in their pups, genetics do not work like that.

Line and inbreeding
There are other aspects of pure breeding which fail to have much appeal either, as far as I am concerned, and one of these is the matter of line breeding. For the uninitiated and to put it in a nutshell, this is the practice of breeding to a particular line or strain, the idea being to fix and perpetuate any desirable features with which that particular line is associated. Unhappily, whilst on this primrose path to one's golden goal, it is also a very easy matter to fix and perpetuate various highly undesirable factors carried by recessive genes of which one had not been aware. Those of cynical outlook will then refer to the activities, which have been going on with so much optimistic hope, as inbreeding. That is if the defects should come to light, which more often than not they fail to do, pedigree breeders being past masters at burying their failures. Line breeding is all very well if accompanied by very heavy culling but is no highway to be trodden by the unwary.

Why breed?
I find longdogs satisfactory. Satisfactory, that is, for my own particular requirements which, I would be the first to admit, are not those of everyone else. With any sort of dog the sort one has must depend very much upon your own requirements. This is true of any working dog but more probably so in the case of a hunting dog, where personal needs and points of view tend to be even more important. This is one of the reasons why the ideal solution to the problem of finding a dog that suits you is to breed your own. Even by following this course one may still sometimes end up disappointed.

Although there are a few breeders who may be relied upon to have for sale exactly what they advertise, there are certain others who are not quite so particular. Added to this is the fact that, even with the very best of faith, when breeding one animal of one breed with one of another genetically there must always be the possibility of something unexpected cropping up in their offspring.

There can be little doubt that the best way of ensuring that you get the dog you feel you require is by acquiring the right sort of bitch, finding a suitable stud and breeding your own litter. But, before proceeding any further, just sit back and give the matter some serious thought and, having done that, think yet again. If you are breeding to provide a puppy for yourself you have then got to decide how you are to going to dispose of the rest. In the normal litter of longdogs you will find that you have probably at least eight whelps. Personally, unless I had had enquiries for a dog of this

Socialising a puppy is vitally important.

breeding, I would put all the male whelps down at birth. These days few people seem to want dogs, the market being almost exclusively for bitches. It may go a bit against the grain to have to get rid of them at this early stage, but to keep them will be to store up trouble for yourself later on. It is easier to put them down before getting to know them well and, believe me, by the time the litter has reached a marketable age, you will know them all extremely well. Another facet of this, which may weigh with the more commercially minded, is that one does not rear a litter of longdog whelps for a pittance. It is a very expensive business without much profit in it even if all goes exactly right, which it seldom does.

Consider for a moment the sort of homes your pups will be going to, it may be going to one of the people, of whom there are too many, who sell or swap the dog the minute it does not measure up to what they consider they require of it? Once a dog gets into this sort of scene it is usually not long before it winds up with its boudoir in the middle of a heap of scrap iron and under some trailer, a rich aroma of fuel oil being all pervading. Or, even worse, it may wind up in the avaricious clutches of some dog dealer, a purveyor of canine misery. With my own pups, I make a point of ensuring that they are going to decent homes and, if such is not on offer, have no hesitation in putting them down. This may seem somewhat draconian to the woolly minded, but there is sound reasoning behind it.

The stud dog

If you still decide to breed, and assuming that the bitch which you have is 100 per cent all right, then the next item on the agenda is to find a suitable stud and the best time to commence your search for whatever paragon you have in mind, is not when you discover your bitch is coming on heat. The father of your future aspirations should have been selected and arrangements made for the use of his services well ahead of the time they will be called upon.

So far I have been mainly thinking in terms of crossbreeding longdogs for, if you want a working dog, it would be difficult to equal such an animal, but it may be possible that you have it in mind to breed some pedigree, purebred longdogs. For this purpose you will have possessed yourself of a registered bitch, either whippet, deerhound, greyhound or saluki or, for that matter, something really way out in the shape of a borzoi, wolfhound, Ibizan hound, Pharoah hound or even a sloughi. You may be under the impression, mistaken as you will discover, that all that you have to do at the appropriate time is to telephone the owner of some suitable stud of that breed. You may well discover that your pious assumptions have been formulated in vain and that your advances will prove futile. I have before me a fairly recent copy of a fieldsports magazine in which there appeared an advertisement which may begin to indicate to you that the way before you is paved with sharp stones and may also show you the sort of reception that you can expect. I quote: 'Deerhounds. Quality puppies available but not as lurcher producing machines. No objection to lurcher enthusiasts genuinely interested in deerhounds. Annual check kept on all stock sold. Pups registered and parvo inoculated.' Well, don't say that you haven't been warned. If this is an advertisement for pups, which presumably they wish to sell, how much more careful are such folk going to be in respect of the services of their precious stud dogs?

Whilst I have every sympathy with those breeders who wish to ensure, to the best of their ability, that their pups will go to the right sort of homes, from the purchaser's point of view I would certainly not want the doubtful privilege of having my dogs checked annually in this way. Life is quite full enough of petty irritations and restrictions as it is without taking on any further commitments of this nature. Neither am I likely to forget the disapproving and stony reception I received when I was looking for a dog to which to put my perfectly reputably bred and registered deerhound bitch. But when I put her to a greyhound, the owner was just as charming and accommodating as it was possible to be in the matter. I may add that I have never, in any way, regretted the decision which I came to then. I wound up with stock worth having rather than things which, although recorded in detail, might have been found wanting in other ways. However, it would not appear that all deerhound owners are quite like the one I approached, for I recently noticed another announcement in the same fieldsports magazine: 'Deerhound at stud. Proven coursing stock, superb specimen.' I think all will agree that this demonstrates an altogether more positive and helpful attitude, but, believe me, in my experience it is unusual.

The only thing is, would you want to breed this way round? Personally I favour the opposite cross – using a greyhound dog on deerhound bitch. I know that this sounds a bit like the chap who was asking his way from where he was to somewhere else in the west of Ireland (or it may have been the north of Scotland or Brittany or Outer Mongolia or some other similar highly civilised but not over sophisticated sort of place, of which a few, thank goodness, still exist). Comes the time-honoured answer. 'Well, in the first place I wouldn't be starting from here'. However, there is a certain method in my madness not because there is any difference in the pups if you breed this way but because you will have to live with the bitch. Providing that you are willing to pay the right sort of price, you can acquire a deerhound, saluki or any other sort of bitch. On the other hand, you may well be able to come by some greyhound bitch which has been retired from the tack and is free to a good home. If you do the latter, as I have said, you may have a certain amount of difficulty in finding a suitable stud. Also, should you have an old and cherished cat, you may well say goodbye to this, for some retired greyhound bitches I have known have been accomplished cat slayers. They are not too backward at disposing of small pet terriers either. Just have a second thought before taking on one of these apparent bargains.

So here I am, on the one hand counselling you to breed your own, and on the other warning you against so doing. Where does the answer lie? I think if you should wish to breed something to your own requirements or to those of your oldest and most trusted friends, then go ahead but, should you be thinking of breeding to make a quick buck while getting a puppy for yourself into the bargain then think again. At the outset, you may just as well give up all hopes of making a fortune or even a bit of beer money for this is a field where, despite rumours to the contrary, very few people break even let alone prosper.

Breeding and rearing
I do not intend to enter into the technicalities of breeding. This side of the matter is already adequately covered in a number of good books to which I have little to add, and Captain Portman Graham's *Mating and Whelping of Dogs* is hard to beat in this field. Any doubts you may have on any of the technicalities can swiftly be resolved by consulting your friendly veterinary surgeon, who will probably look for a few shillings for his advice, but will probably save you pounds in the long run. I would mention that, generally speaking, longdogs are not difficult to breed. Uncomplicated by such problems as habitually plague breeders of things like bull-dogs, with their difficult and ludicrous conformation, the actual process of giving birth is usually straightforward enough. There are sometimes slight mating problems with longdogs but any competent vet will sort things out in this department without a lot of hassle.

Longdog bitches usually produce quite good sized litters but I think it is unwise to seek to rear more than eight. Even with this sort of quantity the bitch will have to be very well fed and the whelps will need to be put on to some sort of supplementary feeding just as soon as they will take it. The best solid food to start them on is scraped beef. This is simple enough to produce: a fair sized piece of stewing steak or shin will do very nicely. The only other item you will need is a sharp knife, the edge of which is then drawn, with a scraping action, over the surface of the beef. This should provide you with a slightly bloody sort of pulp which they will take at quite an early age. I usually start my own litters off with this at between

104

two and three weeks of age and at the same time I get them on to a milk substitute such as Lactol.

Culling should be carried out as early as possible, preferably within the first 48 hours. It goes without saying that weak and deformed specimens should be painlessly put down earlier than this. Should you be selling any of the litter, and reason would seem to dictate that you cannot keep the lot, you will find that bitches sell very much better than dogs. Amongst both lurcher and longdog men the bitches have a better reputation for hunting than the dogs and, from my own observations, I find this to be entirely justified.

Puppies need space and freedom to develop to their full potential.

At one time no one seemed to want bitches which were regarded as being tiresome when in season and very liable to get in whelp. It is said by some that the change of attitude came about as soon as Ovarid came on the market and by means of dosing your bitches with it you could forget about the tiresome sexual drawbacks of the canine female. About the same time spaying became more of a commonplace practice and this had a similar result. However, all this being as it may, we have to face the fact that bitches are in demand where dogs are not. This is not such a bad thing in itself but, in any case, the male issue from longdog crossbreeding does tend to be a bit gangling and rawboned, a physical state which rarely seems to be picked up by the bitches. Whilst this can be something of a shortcoming in the larger sighthounds, it is far from the case with the whippets and their crosses where the male issue often turn into exceedingly useful sorts.

105

Depending, of course, upon what sort of homes they are going to, the pups should be ready to go at about six weeks of age. Some breeders slavishly hang on to them until they are eight weeks old but this is not at all necessary. If ever I am acquiring a pup from another breeder, I will always insist on having it at six weeks old, otherwise no deal. If I could get them even earlier, so much the better. From four weeks of age they should be handled as much as possible and in the company of human beings whenever this can be arranged. This is one of the few occasions when it is a very good thing to have a large family. Kids and pups of this age are remarkably good for one another.

This is the time when the one man, one dog relationship begins to score and, unless you just cannot face the idea, your longdog puppy should never see the inside of a kennel but should be kept with you in whatever dwelling you happen to be inhabiting, for this is when the process of imprinting, so vital to the successful keeping of a longdog, takes place. Apart from this, in these days of barefaced thieving, any dog worth having should be in as secure a location as is possible, for the lowest form of animal life, the dog thief, seems to be on the increase and unfortunately thriving. Also longdogs with deerhound and wolfhound blood are quite formidable watchdogs and their presence inside your dwelling can pay dividends in this way. This may seem like a bit of a contradiction in terms, but a dog inside your house is a much more formidable proposition than one in a kennel outside, a fact of life, which some of my neighbours found out the hard way during Mau Mau days in Kenya.

Imprinting
Mind you, on the matter of imprinting, this is a process which it is possible to carry just that little bit too far. At one time we had in the house a dog which thought it was a human being, a parrot that thought it was a dog, and a cat which, by reason of its preference for inhabiting the inside of the parrot's cage which the bird vacated at the slightest opportunity, obviously thought that it was a parrot. Meanwhile the parrot wandered around the place barking. At different times our household has included anything from cheetahs to porcupines, with usually a sheep or two in and out of the kitchen.

Of course there has to be some sort of differentiation between domestic animals and farm livestock in commercial quantity but I must confess that nothing gives me greater pleasure than to see some old and well-known hen pecking around on the kitchen floor. After all, this is what kitchens must be for, isn't it? What you put into life you get out of it and, although you are not doing any great disservice to your dogs by keeping them in a run at the end of the garden or to your cat when you throw it out of doors last thing at night, you are imposing a very real deprivation upon yourself by denying yourself the pleasure of their company. All the more reason for keeping their numbers small. Just to pursue this particular point a little bit further, I should perhaps mention that amongst some of the companions of my youth it was always held that not only should your longdog, from the time you acquired it (at as early an age as possible) be with you all day (carried inside your shirt as often as not at the start) but also sleep on your bed and on last weeks washing (or maybe last month's washing or even last year's, depending upon how fastidious you happen to be) and, when sleeping on your bed it should be encouraged to do so with it's nose in your armpit. Personally I have never subscribed to this particular practice, mainly for the reason that it has to be rather less than comfortable. There was however, an alternative method of going about the same thing, presumably recommended in the case of the more privileged classes of society – those who possessed a Sunday suit (but not the next class up, who went to work in their Sunday suits and did not have longdogs). This was to take a piece of meat, place it under your armpit and keep it there as long as you felt inclined and then give it to the dog to eat. This, it was counselled, would form a bond between the dog and yourself, as a result of which it would thereafter not stray. I have tried it; my dogs do not stray, but I am not putting QED at the end of it.

—8—

Choosing and Bringing on a Puppy

S O, LET US begin at the beginning and assume that we are about to make our pick of the litter and, to start with, we will look at this from the point of view of having bred the litter. All other things being equal, one would expect to have an earlier sight of a home produced litter than one bred elsewhere, and this is perhaps another reason for breeding your own rather than buying in. The whelps are under your eye from the minute they first start to breathe.

Breeding your own
Just after a puppy is born is an excellent time for making your first appraisal of the sort of dog it is likely to turn into for this is the moment, and it will be little more than a moment, when very frequently the really outstanding pups may be recognised and, should you be so fortunate or so gifted as to possess an eye for such things, it is quite remarkable how a snap judgement at this time can be proven to have been correct later on. This is also the time when the really strong individuals have a habit of showing up. Such an animal was Grendel. It is a habit of mine to take notes of the progress of a litter and the time that I commence these is during the period of parturition, at the exact time that the pups come into

109

the light of day. I have to hand those which I made at the moment that Grendel first drew breath. Within an hour of his first appearing into the world, he had crawled over the top of his dam, who was still giving birth to the rest of the litter, and had wound up somewhere behind her back, meanwhile mewling piteously, albeit with a good deal of force. This I consider to be pretty good going on the part of an hour old whelp. About an hour later he did a repeat performance and, after this, kept up his progress throughout the night at roughly similar intervals.

This pup grew up as a big, strong whelp, later to become a big, strong sapling and finely a big, strong dog. His constitution has never been in the slightest degree of doubt for when he was little over a year old, he managed to stray out on to the road and was hit by a lorry; this broke three of his legs. His owner got him along to the vet with all due haste and all three legs were pinned. At the time I very much doubted whether he would be much use following such a ghastly accident. Had he still been in my possession, I must admit I should have strongly considered the advisability of putting him down there and then. How wrong I would have been was borne out by subsequent events, for he recovered completely in a very short time and since then has proven himself as a single-handed hare killer, taking them in very good style indeed. At the time of writing he is seven-years-old, still going strong, and at the present rate, good for quite a long time to come. On his initial appearance into the world he was so patently obviously one of the right sort that anyone with little or no knowledge of dogs whatsoever, but with a slight degree of commonsense, would have immediately recognised him as a winner.

When one is breeding the greyhound dog to the deerhound bitch a good deal of care needs to be exercised as far as the male whelps are concerned. Whilst it is seldom that a bitch of this cross is other than good, the dogs tend to grow out to be rather too large for the ideal hunting dog and, naturally, the larger they are, the less handy they seem to be.

Dewclaws
The third day after whelping is the time to get the dewclaws off. One hears all the pros and cons as to whether or not this should be done, but most of the reasons given in favour of their retention do not seem to hold much water in my opinion. One hears that they will assist the dog in grooming itself, which seems to be about the most fatuous supposition of all, and I have heard people amongst the lurcher fraternity say that they assist the dog on the turn. I

cannot see them being of very much assistance in these circumstances either. Any dog relying on its dewclaws to fetch it round at speed would not be long in sustaining a torn claw and the sight of one dog with this particular injury will put one clean off any argument for the retention of these appendages very swiftly. Whilst at one time this was an operation which could be carried out by the breeder, it is now one for which it is obligatory to use the services of a veterinary surgeon. Needless to say, the bitch should be removed from the scene of the activities otherwise the skills of a doctor may be required as well as those of a vet.

Gudrun a nine week old deerhound/greyhound that developed into a superb hunter.

Handling the young pup
Young pups should not be handled any more than is strictly necessary during the first three weeks of their lives. For the first week or so their eyes have not opened and even for some time after this they will still not be capable of seeing very much. After three weeks have elapsed, and certainly after four weeks, puppies cannot be handled too much and should be made a good deal of at every opportunity. These are the ones which are going to be easier

to train at a later stage. Give them names now and talk to them a good deal. It is not too early to start getting them used to coming to you when called, training them in the gentlest possible way, of course.

Buying a pup

Now let us examine the situation from a somewhat different aspect – that of potential purchaser. Such a person will, one hopes, be looking for his new longdog pup from a breeder, the bona fides of whom are above reproach. Despite reports to the contrary, such breeders do exist and do not take too much seeking out. Speaking generally, although fewer and further between than those who breed lurchers, longdog breeders are easier to check on and therefore more to be trusted. This may appear to be something of a cynical attitude on my part but lurcher or long-dog breeder is a description which can sometimes be intended to conceal the true identity of a dog dealer, in respect of which gentry I can only counsel caution, the watchword being **'beware'**.

Get a sight of the litter as soon as you are able. No one, other than the breeder, can be expected to see them as they are born, which, as I have mentioned, is the best time to spot the most likely winner, although if you have an eye for a dog, you may well be able to pick out a right one at a few weeks old. Just stand back and have a good look at them for a time, refusing to be hurried in your decision. You will probably see which is the most aggressive. This is the one that a good many of the doggy books will advise you to choose, but forget about this sort of advice for the time being and you will probably, after a short time, be able to discern which is the quickest, liveliest and the most responsive – this is the one to choose. As for looking for long backs, all longdogs have long backs, and bear in mind that I am talking about longdogs, not lurchers. Should none of them suit, do not be afraid to say so. Incidentally, when looking at longdog pups with the idea of making a purchase, ignore all this pretentious rubbish about, 'no time wasters', sometimes inserted as part of an advertisement. My advice would be to make abundantly sure that you do not waste his or her time simply by not bothering to look at the wares of such people. This is the parrot cry of the dog dealer. Any breeder of any sort of stock who is worth his salt will be only too happy to spend time with anyone who is interested in his stock, whether or not a purchase is made. However, having inspected whatever is on offer, either make your bid or for evermore hold your peace. Don't leave saying that you will think

112

about it. Stand your ground and say either 'Yes', or 'No', there and then. No one is going to think less of you for being decisive. But bear in mind, above all, that you are the purchaser with good hard coin of the realm tightly clasped in your sticky paw and he is selling, or at any rate trying to sell.

A strong nine month old puppy.

It is your time that is often being wasted by misleading advertising and, should what is on offer fail to be what the advertisement suggested, you should not be slow to tell the vendor so, always depending of course on how big and nasty he happens to be or, for that matter, how big and nasty you happen to be. If, on the other hand, you should happen to see something which you like, and let's face it this is most often the result of someone telling you that old so and so has a litter of such and such breeding rather than responding to an advert, get the pup away from the litter just as soon as you are able to take it, once it is over the age of 28 days. Keep it in the house with you. Feed it on raw scraped steak. Encourage it to sleep on your bed, on your discarded clothes, anywhere just so long as it is in close contact with you. This way you will imprint it, make it believe that it is a member of your family and, in the process, set you up with a hunting dog which for sheer intelligence, let alone a probable breath-taking performance will leave most lurchers standing. Mind you, when you are doing this make sure that the puppy is not competing with other dogs for your attention, and build a one man, one dog relationship with it.

This is the real relationship of one man and his dog or, if you like, *One Man and His Dog.* The popular television series of this name, excellent though it is, depicts anything but one man and his dog. Let no one be under the impression that any one of the highly sophisticated participants in this incredibly slick and remarkably well produced series of television programmes operates full-time on a one man and his dog basis. The beautifully presented cameos of each of the competitors demonstrates this not to be the case. Believe me, having seen a good deal of life here and there in my travels, the one to one relationship is the only one that really works be it with dogs or wives. Whilst it may seem ripping good fun to have two or three or even more wives, it is a situation which, for most people, only too swiftly palls, one at a time being good fishing, as they say, and one at a time being enough, or sometimes slightly overmuch, for most of us. Many of my African friends, who have had first hand experience of such arrangements will be the first to bear me out in this.

Feeding the pup
With the prospect of a strenuous working life ahead of it, it is absolutely imperative that the longdog pup should have a good start in life, if anything a better one than one might give a lesser breed fed for nothing more strenuous than a gentle amble around the park on Sunday mornings, weather permitting, of course. Well, the old saying which was heard rather more in the past than the present, went something after the style of, 'You can't have a good set of engines without a good sized boiler-room'. This was a favourite quote of the great Tony Galento, the 'Joisey Nightstick', a man who trained on beer and was one of the few to make any sort of showing against the might Joe Louis.

To take this sort of reasoning a bit further, one has to consider the kind of fuel that is to be used under the boilers and, in the case of young pups, this should take the form of easily assimilated protein, the most suitable foods being milk and raw beef. Whilst most longdog mothers are good at the job, a fair sized litter which should be making phenomenal increases in body weight, will be a good deal the better for something to supplement mama's contribution. The pups should therefore be encouraged to take milk in some form or other just as soon as they can be encouraged to lap. Years ago on farms where there was usually plenty of skim milk, this together with barley meal being frequently used as a staple diet for fattening pigs, there was always enough to spare for any pups which happened to be around. Today using skim would be a costly business and this is where milk substitutes are useful. I have used Lactol in recent years and it is as well to get the litter on to this before they are three weeks of age for this is about the time that the bitch's milk will start to dry up.

Within a week after this, they should be taking scraped meat. This is quite easily prepared by literally scraping a piece of meat across the grain with a sharp knife, the resultant bloody pulp usually being readily taken by pups. The fibrous bits which are left over will do nicely for the bitch or might even be the basis of a nourishing stew for yourself if you are hard up, as you probably will be by the time that you have reared a litter of longdog pups. Beef is the most suitable meat for this purpose, although I have reared pups on everything from zebra to buffalo meat. They will probably take mince by the time that they are six weeks old or even before that. If you don't know the butcher too well or perhaps even if you do, select your own piece of meat and get him to mince it. Some butchers' mince contains all sorts of fat and gristle that is not much good to the interiors or young pups. Four meals a day is about right for pups of this age.

If you have money to burn there are numerous tinned puppy foods available, but I would not recommend this as a method of feeding a longdog puppy – its only advantage being convenience. You could also start feeding a puppy on one of the complete dog foods such as Wilsons, this is both convenient and wholly adequate, though being brought up in the old school I still prefer to feed a puppy on fresh meat if possible.

Worm your litter at or about 28 days of age and again at 42 days. Handle the pups as much as you can at all stages and you will have made a start towards producing some useful longdogs.

If you have not sold the pups by six to eight weeks then get them injected, particularly against parvo virus.

—9—

Training

W HEN WORKING WITH longdogs it is well to remember that all dogs are first and foremost creatures of habit. Therefore, whatever you do, certainly at the start, try and ensure that you do it at as near as possible the same time every day and preferably in the same place. Whatever innovation you have in mind, start proceedings off with a slavish repetition of what you were doing the day before, and the day before that, and every day previously. Later on, when your dog is going well, you will discover that, having put up any sort of quarry anywhere the dog will always show signs of interest at that spot. Dwell there a bit and give the immediate area a thorough combing out. Should anything pop up, albeit only a mouse where yesterday or the day before it was something much larger, lay the dog on to it, at the same time thanking providence for small mercies. Probably you will not turn anything up but do not move on before your faithful friend has had an opportunity of making a find. Never be in too'much of a hurry at this stage and whatever appears to sink in, reinforce in any way at your disposal.

Lead training
First things first, however, and in this case it is lead training. There are those who claim that they are able to train a dog without ever having to put it on a lead but these must be pretty gifted persons as

117

Always lead train your longdog as a puppy it is essential not only for control but to aid further training.

well as being the possessors of fairly gifted animals. So for the ordinary run of the mill sort of chap like you or me, lead training it has to be and this can, and should be, started at a comparitively early stage in the dog's life. If you have managed to acquire your pup at six weeks of age then get on with it immediately, for it is something which can be done even in quite a constricted space. Make sure that there are no other dogs around to distract your

118

charge, and use a light lead. I always use the Turner-Richards type of slip lead of Peter Moxon's design for a start and, for that matter, still carry on using them for my older dogs. They are useful pieces of equipment which have the added virtue of being light and taking up a minimum of space when not in use. I usually carry a spare one in my pocket at all times for, if you are amongst dogs for a good part of your time, you never know when one may come in handy. There are some dogs which require the use of a choke chain but the majority of longdogs do not come into this category. I would never make the initial attempt to lead train a longdog pup with a choke chain which would probably do more harm than good by unnecessarily frightening the poor little brute.

A working longdog must be taught to sit/lie and stay for you to adequately control it when hunting.

Sit and down

The longdog usually takes to the lead without much trouble and fairly swiftly. Once this has been accomplished and the pupil is walking nicely by your side, you will be able to progress a bit further. The next thing to instil into the dog's mind is to go down on command. Many trainers will not do this until they have taught the dog to come when called, but I regard this as secondary to going down when required to do so for, as soon as it will sit or lie down, the sooner it is under control and, whatever situation you can see it going into, you will have a means of anchoring it. You may have noted that I have said that the pup should be taught either to sit or lie down, and I have put it this way quite deliberately. There are definite benefits in their going straight into the prone position for they present far less of a profile this way which can sometimes be an advantage. I always train my own dogs this way and have had no cause to regret it.

Stay
The next thing to inculcate in them is to stay on command. Some would-be trainers never seem to master this one and, with some dogs, it can turn into something of a battle of wills but patience and perseverance will usually get you there in the long run. The basic principle when trying to get this one home is, without fail, if it follows you when you walk away from it, as most of them will at first, take it back and repeat the command. Don't carry it there and, above all, even if you are so exasperated as to feel like doing so, don't throw it there. Just put it on a lead, walk it back and go through the whole rigmarole once more.

Come
Once you have the animal going down as directed and then staying there, you can get on with training it to come when called. You will discover that it will learn this with considerable alacrity. In teaching it to come when it is called, do not make the mistake, of shouting at the beast by its name whenever it does something requiring reproof. At such moments as these call it by any name you like (I don't think the offence of using obscene language is still on the Statute Book, so you can let yourself go a bit) but never, never by its own name. So many people do this and then expect the thing to come to them, when it hears the same thing yelled at it. Instead teach it to come to its name, and to your own particular whistle. Longdogs are very much cast in the same mould as many of their owners in that they appreciate a bit of peace and quiet so it is a good thing to condition them to come to a click of the fingers or of the tongue.

Hand signals
Longdogs can also profitably be trained to react to hand signals

both on the lead and off it at a distance. The so-called soundless dog whistle can also be introduced into the programme about now. It is just as easy to go about one's business in a quiet way as a noisy one and you will find that longdogs react better to quietness and calm than to a lot of noisy hullaballoo and shouting. You don't want to scare away the quarry, do you? Nor anything else for that matter, otherwise you would be following a pack of hounds when you could shout as much as you liked at the appropriate time.

One dog stays where placed waiting for a rabbit to bolt while another is controlled by a hand signal.

Retrieving

Do not wait too long before teaching your dog to retrieve for this is something which it is easier to get into their heads at an early age than later on. I have never experienced any difficulties in teaching longdogs to do this. All those I have ever had seemed to do it quite naturally, but having heard of difficulties in this direction which have been experienced by some owners, I should perhaps mention that, from a fairly early age, I run my pups with an old and staid retriever, which can always be relied upon to welcome a jolly game of bringing back anything which is thrown for her. It takes only a very short time for the longdog pups to enter into the game.

121

However, they frequently tire of this amusement fairly quickly and the activity must immediately be brought to a close. If one perseveres and does just a short time at it regularly every day, they will soon have it right. This is the basis of all animal training; absolute regularity and knowing the exact moment that the trainees have had enough. Then a jolly good chase around just to keep things on the right level.

All longdogs should be taught to retrieve.

It is probable, however, that your establishment will not run to such a helper and you will have to manage on your own. Most young dogs will be more than keen to enter into a game of fetch and carry and this can be developed into full scale retrieving as a rule. I have had several longdogs, both pure blooded deerhounds and deerhound/greyhound hybrids, all of which have been perfect retrievers. These have always been dogs which I worked on their own.

Once your longdog will bring quarry back to hand, be very careful about running it with other dogs, particularly terriers. I will make no excuses for reiterating that this is the best way to ruin any longdog. Terriers are jealous hunters and whilst they have their uses in putting things out of cover, they can be relied upon to

122

dispute any kill. The result will be that your carefully trained longdog, which until then has been behaving impeccably, will start biting the heads off of everything it kills and, if you do not take the hint, will excel itself by consuming its quarry instead of bringing it back to you.

Jumping

Your dog will not be a great deal of use to you if it stops dead at every obstacle it finds in its path and waits for you to come along to lift it over, and so it must be taught to jump. This is another area of training which can be commenced at an early age. Whenever I have a litter of pups, I house them in such a way that there is a board in the doorway of wherever they are lodged, so that the bitch can get in and out at will but the whelps are prevented from following her. I also arrange matters so that as the youngsters grow and get stronger, the board will be sufficiently low for them to get over it. This serves two useful purposes; as soon as they are physically able, they will make every effort to surmount the obstacle in their path and, at the same time, it provides a handy means of checking the rate of progress of the individual pups.

This is where things are made so much easier should you have been fortunate enough to breed your own pups, but you may well

A saluki/greyhound clearing a five bar gate with ease.

have had to buy in, in which case although this part of the proceedings will not be quite so simple to carry out, the same principles still apply. The ideal situation is to have some sort of a corridor, perhaps between two fences in a garden or some similar place. Anything of this nature will do, just so long as your pupil cannot escape either sideways or backwards. Do not be overambitious to begin with and start him or her off on something quite modest over which it can almost climb and gradually increase the height of the obstacle as progress is made. You will find that the majority of longdogs, particularly those with some deerhound blood, are natural jumpers and will take a delight in so doing. Try to ensure that they clear their fences clean and do not touch them as they go over, for sooner or later they are going to encounter barbed wire and the more daylight that there is between them and it the better.

When they get to the stage of tackling barbed wire the best way of getting them used to it is to lay an old sack, or failing this, your jacket over the top strand and encouraging your charge to go over at this point. Having accomplished it a time or two in this way, he or she will not be long in grasping the general idea. It is possible to progress from this stage to the clearing of quite high fences and walls but, unless you wish to go in for canine athletic events, a pursuit of dubious worth, there would not seem much necessity to push this aspect of training much further.

By now, if your longdog has been trained correctly, it should go down on command, stay where placed, come when called, retrieve to hand and be able to pursue its quarry undeterred by any normal farm fences. Now is the time to enter it to quarry.

—10—

Management and Feeding

ON THE MATTER of canine health I do not consider that this merits a chapter on its own. It is best dealt with either in one paragraph or in a complete volume about nothing else. On this particular subject I would reckon that as long as you keep your dog's inoculations up to date, worm it in autumn and spring and, if it is a bitch, when it gets in whelp, exercise it adequately, feed it properly and take it to your vet whenever there is anything amiss with it, there is not much more to be said on the subject; on the other hand there is also an awful lot, a book's length in fact, but you would still need your vet. On the subject of vets, I would say that the best course is to find someone who suits you and stick to him. When in doubt, go to him for advice. Being basically a bit of a yokel, I tend to use the old fashioned horse and cattle vet rather than the proprietors of small animal practices who are probably better with cats, Pekingese and poodles than they are with working dogs.

Feeding adult dogs
I have always found that, for feeding longdogs, beast and sheep paunches are just about ideal and the best way to obtain these is straight from the slaughterhouse. However, these days, we are so beset with EEC Regulations, all of which seem to be for the greater protection of the weak-minded, that buying green tripe of this kind

has become well nigh impossible and most owners will have to use some sort of substitute.

A good many people are turning to complete meal substitutes such as Vitalin and Wilsons. These are not at all bad in their way and, as well as being fairly economical, are clean and easy to feed. I must confess that I am never quite happy about them, though. This may well be merely due to inborn prejudice but I like to see a dog getting some of its natural food, meat, down its throat. My own dogs are fed on one of these complete foods but they get a fair amount of steak trimmings and other bits of waste meat that I manage to come by as well.

In prewar days, when gamekeepers were usually provided with a dog maintenance allowance of miniscule proportions on most estates, they fed the gun dogs in their care on barley meal boiled up with a few rabbits which were flung in, paunches and skins and all, sometimes supplementing this with a nauseous looking dog food, which despite its appearance, was nourishing enough, named 'Crappo', a fairly descriptive name, I always used to think. Hardworking gun dogs appeared to do very well on this sort of mixture, which as nearly as I can, I duplicate today with so-called complete dog food and a few meat scraps. The more meat, whatever it is, that you can give them, the better. Another good argument for not being overdogged. Avoid tinned dog foods if you can; they tend to cause dogs to scour and are very expensive in comparison to the alternatives.

Kennelling
Although I seem to have made a good deal of keeping your dog or dogs in the house and am a very firm advocate of this myself, I have not closed my mind on this score to such an extent that I am unable to see that this is not, in some cases, possible. This is when you may have to think about kennelling. This should be the best that you can afford and should provide ample space for the dog to be in weathertight and dry surroundings with a bed well off the floor, out of the way of draughts, as well as something in the shape of an out of door run, preferably roofed and preferably with a concrete, easily cleansed floor.

I am not in favour of dogs being housed in kennels in multiples of more than two and two compatible dogs at that. One must be ultra careful about this aspect of the matter wherever terriers come into the equation for all sorts of hidden fires lurk unseen within these tiny breasts. A friend of mine has recently lost a very good terrier bitch by kennelling it with a lurcher bitch. He had owned both of them for about seven years and there had never been a hint of trouble before. The lurcher bitch has become savage since the incident and will probably have to be put down. Double kennelling could have been the only cause of all this difficulty. Therefore, single kennelling if at all possible and never, never more than two to a kennel. With three or more, sooner or later, ganging up will occur – result death.

Do not put your kennels at the end of the garden but keep them as close to your dwelling as you can. There are dog thieves about who need nothing in the way of encouragement and, from all the cases of dog theft that I have unhappily encountered, a dog once stolen, seems to be pretty near irrecoverable.

Exercise
Whether you keep your longdog in the house or a kennel it will need to be kept fit. It is no good taking it out hunting once a week and expecting it to be in peak condition if the other six days it is lying about in or out of the house. Not only will it not be up to the job in hand but it could be irreparably damaged.

Take it out every day for a combination of road walking and running and you will have a fit and well muscled dog that will be up to the rigours of a day or nights hunting. If you have some woodland nearby this can be very useful for getting the dog to run without too much exertion on your part, it will busy itself hunting up rabbits and squirrels and keep itself in pretty good trim. If you want to give it some real speed work take two dogs to some open space and hand slip them to someone waiting a few hundred yards away.

—11—

Hunting

THIS IS WHERE we come to the subject which most of us regard as the purpose of having a longdog, that of hunting. Having reached the point when the dog's training has progressed sufficiently the time has come to enter it to quarry. In recent times not a very great deal seems to have been said about this aspect of having a hunting dog. In former days, when hounds were employed to hunt just about any variety of game, every dog handler must have followed some sort of set plan, but today, for instance, greyhounds are used, without many exceptions, either for organised coursing or on the track, so the ultimate goal of any sort of training is rather different from that which existed in years gone by.

Today is the day of the specialist and this applies to hounds of the chase, those used for hunting, those used for pest control and so on. It is doubtful whether anyone engaged in full-time rabbit control would want anything much larger than a whippet, whereas a person who has the job of coping with a fox problem would go in for something rather larger. Whatever the eventual aim, however, general principles in regard to entering to quarry remain the same.

Rabbit
In most instances the sapling will first be entered to rabbit and whether the dog is to be used mainly for lamping or for other forms of hunting, it is better started off in the daylight. At this stage, and

129

this stage only, I would advocate taking out more than one dog at a time. In this way the young one will see what it is all about and will soon seek to emulate its seniors. The best sort of place in which to make a start becomes progressively more difficult to find in today's ever more developed and ever more cultivated countryside, and that is a good patch of brambles, which, unless they have been grossly overhunted as is frequently the case near to built up areas, can usually be relied upon to hold a rabbit or two. The best way of getting the rabbits into the open is with the help of a few good terriers. Like everything else in life this is not altogether without its snags, and it is a stage at which you are going to have to be very careful indeed. The reason for this is the one which I have already mentioned, namely that terriers, or at least any terriers worth having, are possessive hunters, which will dispute a kill quite ferociously. This is likely to have one of two effects in the instance we have under consideration. Either it will put off your young entry altogether or it will turn him or her into a similarly savage disputant of the catch. If persisted in, this can quickly have the effect of turning your future filler of the pot, your convertor of coney to casserole, into a tiresome consumer of that which he catches. Having wrested the kill away from the terriers, it will use its superior speed to carry the catch away to some inaccessible spot, where it will swiftly devour it. I have seen a three-month-old deerhound hybrid, take a moorhen away from an old hunting ginger tom cat and swallow the bird whole, the head going down first. All that could be seen after a second or so were the two moorhen feet, one protruding from each side of the dog's mouth. Not an episode to be encouraged.

A rabbit is bolted from a patch of reeds.

Perhaps a less risky way of bolting the game is to poke about in the bushes with a long stick, getting well into the undergrowth yourself and stamping around with your boots a bit. Something which I remember having instilled into me by an old gamekeeper when I went bush beating as a lad was that you always poke with your stick; you never thresh the bushes with it. A rabbit will bolt from the end of a stick poked at it but will often remain in cover to be beaten to death by anyone hammering away at the bush with his cudgel. This is not the sort of job, I may add, for your blue jeans, trainer shoe clad operator, but rather for Derby tweed trousered, hob nailed booted sorts. So long as one keeps uppermost in one's mind the various problems which can arise, this type of work is very valuable at this stage in the proceedings. It is a form of hunting to which the longdog is well suited and provides healthy exercise for both man and dog.

Run rabbit run.

Bolting rabbits with ferrets is another quite good way of providing the necessary quarry, but just make sure that your dog is broken to ferret before you indulge in this type of sport. Should one of your own dogs kill one of your ferrets, this is sufficiently vexatious, but if you should have taken your promising potfiller along to a place where someone else is using his ferrets, probably the apples of his eye, and your pride and joy just happens to give one of them a terminal nip, a situation is created whereby mayhem and perhaps even murder may result. In any case it is no bad thing to acquaint your dog with this sort of work at a fairly early age. Even though your dog may appear to have been broken to ferret satisfactorily at home, matters may assume rather different proportions on the first occasion your dog meets a ferret face to face as it emerges from some rabbit hole. And particularly so if a

Ferreting in North Yorkshire.

rabbit has just bolted and your dog has been set on to it with some
degree of encouragement.

Now is also a good time to dissuade him for once and for all from
sticking his nose down rabbit holes and snuffling about down there.
No self respecting rabbit is going to bolt under circumstances such
as these and will stay to ground preferring to be eaten alive by the
questing ferret than to face the large and ferocious animal which
lurks upstairs. All this side of entering is made very much easier

132

should you have ferrets of your own. Two or even one will be enough. A single trustworthy old hob can be very useful when training new entrants for it is improbable that such a beast will lose his head should things go a bit wrong at any stage of the proceedings. Quite apart from this, ferrets in general, and nice old polecat hobs in particular, are very pleasant creatures to have around.

Legging rabbits makes their carrying easier.

So let us assume that your longdog has been entered to rabbit under conditions of daylight and that it is able to latch on to this rapidly moving, jinking quarry as it dashes from one patch of cover to the next. It is not without good reason that coursing greyhounds

133

are kept severely away from rabbit for, if anything is going to make them run cunning, this is it. It has been mentioned that longdogs, as opposed to lurchers, are not so good on the pick up. Those who hold this opinion have very obviously never seen a whippet in action. On the other hand, it may be found that the odd deerhound blooded longdog may not pick up a fleeting quarry as well as do some others, but this assumes a position of some insignificance as the uncanny reasoning powers of the longdog of this breeding comes into play. Once they get used to the game, you will discover they always seem to be just where the quarry is going to bolt and will snap it up before it has gone a couple of yards.

Not always being one to slavishly practise what I preach, I sometimes run my old deerhound hybrid bitch Gudrun with a bobbery pack on Sunday mornings. Nine times out of ten she will catch the rabbit in the face of four terriers, two whippets and a lurcher bitch from a very distinguished kennel. Why? Simply for the reason that she is always in the right place at the right time.

Having pleaded guilty to not always practising what I preach, I should perhaps just mention that if you are determined to follow my practice rather than my advice, just try to ensure that your longdog does not manifest his state of boredom with pack hunting by getting into the habit of retrieving terriers rather than rabbits. A deerhound dog which I bred and, perhaps unwisely, gave to my daughter as a pet was walked by her in Greenwich Park since she was living in South East London at the time. He became only too adept at retrieving any other dog which he saw there, neatly securing the unfortunate beasts by the collar and dragging them back to his owner. A useful accomplishment should you happen to be in the dog stealing business, but otherwise not without a certain degree of embarassment.

Rat
At this stage in the entering of your dog to quarry generally, a worthwhile digression may now take place. Should you know of any nearby location where there may be a few rats, try to sublimate your quite correct feelings about them, and do not proceed thither with a sharp terrier or two in order to take them out with a minimum of fuss and a certain amount of satisfaction. By all means take a terrier but also take your longdog for there is no better way of sharpening up any dog than by letting it have a go at rats and it will do its hunting instincts no end of good. Whippets in particular are natural ratters and the best of them are a good deal better than an average terrier. I have had excellent sport recently using two

Always take care when working terriers and lurchers together.

good terriers together with a whippet bitch in an old rat-infested building not far from where I live. This particular whippet had not encountered rat before and, when one of the creatures bolted from under a building she took it rather clumsily in the middle of the

135

adjacent field. So bad a hold did she take of it that it bit her rather badly, as only a rat can do. Nevertheless she killed the thing, since which time she has not only been absolute mustard on rats, taking them and killing them with a bite in far better style than many a terrier, but also has been much keener to rabbit, and has therefore become an absolutely first rate hunter in consequence.

Lamping

Once your dog has started to catch rabbits in the daylight, your thoughts may now turn to using him for lamping. As you may have gathered, as a form of sport I do not regard this activity any too highly but I must add that, should anyone have a rabbit problem, lamping properly carried out is probably the best available means of dealing with it that they are likely to find at the present time. In the days before myxomatosis hit the thriving rabbit population of these isles, the majority of farmers, smallholders, foresters and gardeners suffered a great deal from the depredations of these creatures but were not able to hunt them with the aid of a lamp in the accepted sense of the term as we know it. The main reason for this was that the lightweight battery had yet to be developed, but also many of the farms in those days were of the tenanted variety and the estate owners thought only in terms of semi-domesticated reared pheasants. Nothing must be done which might in any way be interpreted as being in the least way detrimental to these fowl, which meant that anyone hunting during the hours of darkness would incur the wrath of the gamekeepers and the displeasure of his landlord. Not to mention the unwelcome attention of the village policeman, whose pedal cycle, whilst not having the speed of the modern patrol car, was considerably less noticeable and did not carry a blue light.

I know all about the provisions of the Ground Game Act of 1880 but am also aware of the way in which the rights of tenant farmers were eroded on a large number of estates. That the same mentality exists today is demonstrated by the attitude of some of the game shooting fraternity but differing economic circumstances have drawn the teeth of most of the shooting syndicates, many of whose members must hanker for what, in their view, must have been the good old days. There are more ways of killing a cat than choking it with cream and there were just about as many ways of getting rid of a recalcitrant tenant farmer, despite the security of tenure supposedly afforded by various Agricultural Acts. Had it not been for the availability and, more important, the legality of the gin trap, the rabbit problem would have assumed even greater proportions.

Lamping with a deerhound/greyhound cross greyhound/whippet.

Should you wish to indulge in lamping, it goes without saying that your first requirement will be a lamp and you could not do better in this respect than go along to a firm where the business is run by fieldsports people well aware of all the problems and snags which are likely to be experienced by the novice and only too happy to give practical advice. You will thus be acquiring not only a lamp but also a very great deal of useful advice; two for the price of one, in fact. From my own personal experience, I would advise against purchasing anything too high powered for a start. You do not really want to light up some place a mile away for the very good reason that there is a limit to the range of vision of the human eye. Added to this consideration there is also the indubitable fact that the more powerful the lamping outfit, the heavier will be its weight and the higher will be its cost.

Lamping a rabbit.

The type of lamping outfit I have always found to be perfectly adequate is one which consists of a 55 watt quartz halogen lamp with a 12 volt rechargeable 6.5 amp gel battery. Such an outfit will provide you with 250,000 candlepower's worth of light, which is quite a lot of candles to fit into one small lamp, and will give you something over one hour of continuous lamping. There are also high intensity spotlights on the market and very tempting they are too, many of them with evocative names. I should think twice before obtaining one of these, for in my own experience and that of many of my friends who do a great deal more in the way of night hunting than I do, the beam, whilst being long-carrying and brilliantly illuminating, is a good deal too narrow for an ideal hunting lamp.

I am assuming that you will have obtained all the necessary

permissions (in writing for them to be effective) before going onto any land you intend to hunt. So now you have a dog which has demonstrated that he knows what a rabbit is and what to do with it and above all, is a reliable retriever of his catches, this being an absolute necessity in a lamping dog. You also have a new and efficient lamping outfit and permission to hunt. The battery is charged and your immediate inclination will be to rush out to the nearest field and commence operations. But restrain yourself for a moment. In the words of the old song: 'Watchman, what of the night?'

Like the watchman, it will now pay you to regard the great outdoors. One thing will be fairly certain; it will be too early an hour at which to venture forth. There are two sorts of novice lampers to avoid. One type sally forth as soon as darkness falls. The second sort are even worse for they tend to set about their business soon after the pubs chuck out, until which time they have been sitting in licensed premises, clad in camouflaged garments, wellies turned down the regulation three inches at the top and their lurchers lying at their feet, each of them cocking his eye up from time to time with the expression of 'How much longer, O Lord?'

Both the first or second sort can be fairly readily recognised and fairly accurately categorised in that the first sort's camouflage jacket will be a bit newer and gaudier and the obligatory white socks showing above the tops of the wellies may be a bit cleaner. Probably, having gained the field of action, the first sort may make a bit better showing than the second in that, although his 'prentice feet will fall over every obstacle in his path, he will not come down with quite such a bang as those befuddled with alcohol. They will have one other thing in common, in that on the morrow, they will be boasting to all their mates that they went lamping last night and took some unlikely number of rabbits. The number will assume various totals but seldom be less than about 30, for which they had a ready purchaser who took the lot and that is why they do not have the odd couple available for old Bill, who would dearly like to taste a field rabbit just to remind him of all the hundreds that he used to take in a net all those years ago. Something about the blind leading the blind comes to mind.

Having regarded the state of the night, bearing in mind the awful examples I have quoted, take another look at it and try to form some opinion of what it is going to be like by about two o'clock tomorrow morning. If by then the moon has disappeared, or if there will be sufficient cloud about to obscure it totally, there may just be a chance of the night being right. If it is blowing at least force seven it may well be on. If there are a few drops of rain being lashed at you by the wind, it is probable. So, go to bed; set your alarm clock for 2 a.m. and the minute it goes off, get on your feet, put on a thick jersey and your old donkey jacket, put your longdog on its lead and get along to your rabbiting pitch. By then you may well find that the moon is shining, the wind has dropped and it is a clear and peaceful night, in which case, go back home, make yourself a cup of cocoa with or without a good slug of rum in it, appreciate the beauties of the hour and either go back to bed, putting it all down to experience, or go for a nice long walk and appreciate what, mercifully, few others will be there to share with you – a dead world.

On the other hand it may just happen that the night is as black as pitch, the wind has risen and the rain, although sparse, is hitting you in the face like small shot. Then get moving, for this is your night. If you can walk as far as your scene of operations, so much the better, but if you have to get there by taking a vehicle, put it well off the road when you get there, preferably in some position where it is unlikely to be seen, before approaching your pitch. Although you have permission to hunt, it is still tiresome to have to answer stupid questions from well meaning police constables and gamekeepers at this hour of the night. Not that you are likely to encounter either under the circumstances which I describe, but, as always in this life, it is just as well to be prepared for the very worst eventualities.

So, after all this preamble, you have arrived at your destination for the night, or, at any rate, what is left of it, which, if things go right, you will find quite long enough. Your dog will be at your side on its lead but, just one moment, what sort of lead is it on? I know that a famous artisan hunter advocates using no lead at all, but rather to hold your dog by a length of baling twine looped through its collar, but I never follow this practice myself for two reasons: The first one is that I hate the feel of baling twine in my hand, as will you should your dog pull a bit on the sight of his quarry. The other reason why I would never think of doing this is that I hate to run any sort of working dog in a collar. I know that it does not frequently happen, but should you get either longdog, lurcher or terrier caught up by its collar, you will be likely to wish that you had never run it with one on. In the case of a terrier going to earth, it can be utterly disastrous should one get its collar hung on to an underground snag. It is perhaps slightly less disastrous to have your dog, whatever it may be, hung up by its collar when above ground but it may still prove to be fatal. So I would advise you not to run your dog with a collar on.

Lamping can provide a good haul of rabbits.

I would make only one exception to this rule and that is if you are running a dog specifically against fox and the dog is one that is liable to be bitten, when a wide greyhound type of collar can save its jugular and carotid to some extent. However, if you are foxing with

141

any sort of longdog, as opposed to a lurcher, particularly a longdog with a fair amount of deerhound blood, you will not need to worry unduly on this score for most of these dogs, given the chance and a bit of encouragement, are fox killers, and I mean killers. One bite from those massive jaws in the right place, which they seem soon to learn to find, crushes neck, thorax, heart and ribs in one almighty vice-like crunch.

To get back to leads, should you contemplate going lamping, then a slip lead is a highly desirable asset. There are a very large selection of all kinds of running dog and terrier leads and collars. These include all kinds of slip leads; some have fancy toggle handles with bolts on the collar that are withdrawn by means of a cord running up the lead itself. A single version of the double coursing slip, in fact. This is very good in its way, but to my mind a bit like taking a sledge hammer to crack a nut. Then there is the sort with a spring loaded toggle on one side and these are very good, being used by many of the most practical of lampers, men who rely upon this for a good part of their livings. My own choice is a very simple affair, which has no spring loaded or moving parts but which relies upon the simple slipping of a thong through a ring. I find this sort by far the fastest sort of slip lead in action, the lightest to carry and the cheapest to buy, and with no moving parts to go wrong.

So here we are, on the stubble or what is more likely the winter sown wheat or barley, and ready to go. Switch on your light and have a quick look around the field, just to see if there is anything there, and, if it is, its bearing. Then dowse your light smartly and get yourself and your dog into what you consider to be a strategic position with the wind blowing from the direction of the quarry towards you. If it is blowing crossways, no great matter, but try to avoid putting yourself anywhere where the wind might be blowing from you to the game. Approach your quarry as stealthily as is possible (this is another way in which you ought to be one up on the chap who has left the pub half an hour before he starts lamping). When you reckon that you are about the right distance away from it, switch on your lamp. If all has gone according to plan you should immediately see a rabbit, or perhaps rabbits, in your beam. This is the moment for which you have been waiting. Slip your longdog. Keep the quarry in your beam and leave all else to the dog which, if it has been properly trained and entered, will run down the beam, take the rabbit and retrieve it to hand. Alternatively it will miss the rabbit and return to heel immediately. This is something that must be instilled into every lamping dog for the last thing that you want is an animal which, not having killed, will hunt around, putting down everything within sight.

It is just worth mentioning that, once you have had a successful night's lamping, do not be too eager to return to the same spot and try again for another few weeks, for rabbits will very quickly become lamp shy. Hares are even worse, in fact all quarry beasts are quick to learn that lights at night spell trouble and they act accordingly.

Fox

So much for lamping. As a way of getting rid of large numbers of rabbits it is very effective, but, as a sport it has a fairly low rating in my book. However, before I leave the subject, there is one species other than rabbit which affords a prime target for the lamper and his longdog. I use the term longdog advisedly for to deal effectively with a fox most rabbiting lurchers are to my mind a touch on the small side. For this sort of work you are going to need at least a 26″ dog, preferably with a large dash of deerhound in its makeup. Once such a dog develops the knack of doing it, he will make very short work of a fox, which, as anyone who has first hand knowledge of them will know, can be a very savage creature indeed and possesses a very useful and sharp set of teeth. Mind you, if you start destroying any small portion of the vast numbers of foxes which there are in this country, you will very quickly discover that you are attracting the wrath of a very diverse cross-section of the local population.

You will find that, should you let yourself be brought to their notice, anti-fieldsports people, hunt saboteurs, the RSPCA, Masters of Foxhounds, Hunt Supporters Clubs, and a host of others will be doing their upmost to stop your activites albeit for very different reasons. This will be despite the fact that you will do the job much more efficiently than it could otherwise be carried out, as well as a good deal more humanely. I find the greyhound/deerhound cross to be reliable on foxes, reliable in that they kill their quarry without much trouble or needing much in the way of assistance.

My greyhound/deerhound bitch, Gudrun, has developed a knack of taking and despatching a fox with one enormous bone-shattering bite. She has sustained a few sundry cuts and abrasions whilst in the process of finding out how to do it, but these days it is every ball a coconut. I doubt very much whether many of the collie blooded lurchers possess the sheer jaw power to do this, good as they often are in other ways. Given a little while to settle

A deerhound/greyhound with a vixen that proved no match for such a powerful dog.

themselves to the job, most longdogs will deliver one killing bite, also they have the necessary strength in their neck to complete matters with a vertebrae dislocating shake or two, should this be necessary. You will witness much the same sort of action should you ever have the misfortune to discover that you are the owner of a dyed-in-the-wool dog killer.

Not many people find themselves in this unhappy position but, for my sins, I did so with one dog I had. His most spectacular performance in this respect was to break open the door of my car, in which I had been sure he was secure, in order to seize and slay an unfortunate dog which walked by. Just to make perfect his dastardly act, he chose to commit this sort of mayhem in the middle of a pedestrian crossing on the busy main street of the town near which I was living at the time. I must admit that I took the coward's way out and, dragging him off the cadaver, hurled him into the back of the car and made off with all speed. I tried every means at my disposal to break him of this horrid habit but to no avail. Despite the most severe punishments, he continued to manifest every sign of satisfaction at what he had done and became such a nuisance that I had to put him down as the only way to curb his murderous machinations. A perfect dog in every other way.

Killing foxes is of course a different proposition altogether and one which under the right circumstances should be encouraged. This is the only species which my old bitch treats in this way. She retrieves hares and rabbits to hand without destroying them and leaves alone cats, ferrets and farm livestock such as cattle, sheep and fowls. Just as they are natural killers of any species to which you enter them, the deerhound crosses are easily dissuaded from tackling anything you wish to be left alone. This is where they seem to differ to a marked extent from salukis.

No right-minded person can possibly doubt that in this country there are far too many foxes at present. In this context I speak generally, for, in the fell country of the north of England, although most of the rural inhabitants would be quick to agree that vulpine numbers are excessive, they do, at least, exercise some degree of control over them, which is more than is being done over the rest of this country. Foxhunts admittedly have their problems; beset with motorways, electric railways and various sorts of housing and industrial development in all directions, more country is being denied to them. If this were not enough, more land has turned from grass to arable than was the case prior to 1939, and more owners and occupiers of agricultural land have been got at by the anti-hunting fraternity. Nevertheless, you will discover that hunts

145

which take less than ten foxes in a season, of which there are many will be the first to shout 'Vulpicide'.

So, if you find that you are taking a few foxes, so ensuring that your own livestock will have that little bit less persecution, I would advise you to keep fairly quiet about it if you have a local hunt, despite the fact that the performance of your longdog over a few nights has notched up a take of fox in excess of the total taken by half a dozen nearby foxhunts in a season. Pelts are worth taking sometimes, just depending on the market and, according to Brian Plummer, there is a fairly steady trade in fox carcases amongst those of Oriental origins.

Before leaving the subject of fox, I should point out that there are some dogs which will never have a go at fox and should you discover that you are the possessor of one of these, either just forget about fox or get yourself another dog – one which is more eager in this respect.

Having disposed of the general considerations surrounding the hunting of various sorts of quarry on a lamp let us look again at hunting by the light of day. Well, only just by the light of day I should perhaps say, for the best time to get out and about with your longdog is, to my way of thinking, just as day is breaking. Apart from hunting, this is the best time of the day in any case. When I see foxhounds and beagles meeting at around midday for what can only amount to an afternoon hunt, it makes me quite sorry for them. (However since any really enthusiastic foxhunter must also go in for cub hunting, for which purpose hunt servants and followers are up and about at crack of dawn, they certainly have the opportunity of learning better ways.) Their loss is our gain.

Dawn is the time of day of the hunter and of the conscientious gamekeeper. Mind you, if a gamekeeper is completely committed to his way of life, he is likely to be up and about at just about every hour out of the 24. But, just in the same way as the lamper, don't go over the self same route every time that you venture abroad. Quarry of all kinds is quick to become educated as to the habits both of man and his dogs. At this hour you are likely to find the odd rabbit which has stayed out to feed just that little bit too far from home, and your longdog, if he has been trained properly, and has been given the opportunity to sharpen up his wits and work out distance and angles for himself, will not be slow to take advantage of each situation as it occurs. Your dog, and possibly you yourself should you have become at one with nature, will at this early hour still be able to smell the scent of the hare, just as you will sometimes get the whiff of the fox which has passed that way.

146

Very few other people will be about particularly at break of day in the middle of summer, but you will not want to hunt at this time of the year as your quarry species are producing their young or have done so and the offspring are trying to find their feet. This is the period of the year when the intrepid airgunner takes his toll of rabbits but a few weeks old and with carcases that will feed nothing but his empty ego. It is also the period of the year when the pseudo-lurchermen will be about taking their dogs around in their beat-up vans so as to be able to slip them at pregnant doe hares and half grown leverets, later boasting about the number of 'hares' that Fly and Flint and company have taken that day, not producing the pathetic carcases which they have left to rot in the fields as a sign of their complete and utter lack of any sense of rightness or decency. But you are a longdog man; you will not wish to do this sort of thing, but will be out for the sheer joy of being where you are and to enjoy the world and its sights and smells and noises, all for you and you alone.

Clothing

Fortunately you can still be out sufficiently early to savour the day at its best in the autumn days when the corn has been cut and the game is ready to be taken. Not at four o'clock, it is true, but early enough not to be vexed by too many other persons in your path and figuratively under your feet. Now walk cannily; approach your favourite spots for quarry with the wind in your face. Go silently and do not be seen. This is when you need to think about your feet, and not only where you are putting them and how you are putting them there, but also about what you are wearing on them.

Perhaps you favour the turned down wellies, which always seem to be the style of the Bedlington/whippet afficianado. Personally I find wellies, in any shape or form, whether in green or black or even the new fashionable shade of brown, just a bit too hampering for they are such vulnerable articles, prone to be torn or punctured by every bramble patch to which one comes and into which one must be prepared to leap, should the dog mark to them. This is where a good, stout pair of leather boots come into their own. Most people who wear them in preference to wellies, seem to prefer those with rugged Commando-type rubber soles. They are very good, there is no doubt, but I favour those with leather soles, well nailed with triple hobs. It is true they do ring out a bit on metalled road surfaces, and they do make the gravel crunch that little bit more, all of which tends to advertise your presence, but I do not frequent such surfaces much, spending more of my time in the fields and woodlands where surfaces are less resilient. But either sort are good and will give you a greater feeling of confidence than the most expensive rubber-uppered footwear going. Keep them well cleaned and well greased and you have sound and well bedded-in footwear for a very long time.

As well as moving about as silently as possible, it is also better if you do not advertise your presence in other ways and this does not mean having to wear so called camouflaged clothing at all times. Such garments can delude the unknowledgeable, who might imagine they have the property of rendering their wearers invisible. Far from it, for whilst they can be quite useful in this respect (when taken as part of a general scheme of camouflage,) when worn on their own, at times they only too well render their wearers the more conspicuous. The prime and classic time for this is in the darkness of the night.

Back in 1940, when such clothing was first introduced in its form as the Dennison Smock, whilst we usually wore them by day, the one time that we learnt to leave them at home was when going out on a night patrol when ordinary khaki battledress was better, and a dark jersey even better still. That was until we started operating in winter in the Appenines when white was de rigeur in the snow both day and night. Mind you, the sight of a half dozen snow-suited figures emerging from the vault of the Famillia Monteverdi in Arielli graveyard in the middle of a January night was a sight to put the Hammer House of Horror in the shade. This was where we lay up during the day in our strongpoint and from which we set off at the witching hour on a hunting expedition of our own, the quarry being the men of the Panzer Grenadiers, alive being preferable to dead for live men talk and tell you their inmost thoughts and, more important, the dispositions of their forward defence lines.

A very important part of any system of camouflage is to break up the outline of the object to be camouflaged, in this case yourself. Your head is the part that will give you away every time if you do nothing about it. So, if you do not want to be too noticeable, wear headgear of some kind, preferably such as will throw some shade over your face. If you want to make a thorough job of it, alter the appearance of your face. Paint it; grow a beard – but not a skimpy designer effort or Collier de Barbe, but a real humdinger of a chest protector; it will also keep the winter's chills away from you a bit. Just observe in detail the next pigeon shooter or wildfowler that you see, peering out of his hide, complete with camouflaged jacket and the obligatory woolly hat. What stands out a mile? His honest, shining countenance, blazing forth there like a full moon on a frosty night. Take note, take heed, and learn thereby.

Every time you do not wish anyone or anything to know you are there, do not rely too much upon your latest camouflaged suiting, but seek out the dead ground. You may become so good at doing this that one day you may find yourself doing as successful deer stalkers do, going flat on your belly up the bed of a stream in mid winter with the water going in at your collar and coming out via your boots. One thing never to worry about in such circumstances is the possibility of taking cold, for your strenuous activities will surely obviate anything of this nature.

Many a hare is walked over so effective is their use of camouflage and the lie of the land.

Hare
So far I have not made any mention of the quarry which most people associate with the longdog – the hare. These creatures which not so long ago existed in large numbers in most parts of the country have, like most other forms of wildlife, become casualties of some of the marvels of modern science as applied to the present day methods of agriculture. The result has been that, where in former times there were large hare populations, today there are frequently none.

But is this the whole story? Recent work by the Game Conservancy points to what appears to be the real culprit in the

149

matter and that is the fox. The Conservancy's investigations into the problem have been conducted with the complete thoroughness and meticulous attention to detail which one has come to associate with this body and have extended to laboratory analysis of fox faeces as well as electronic tagging. It has been, by these and other means, proved beyond doubt that immense numbers of leverets and even adult hares are taken by Charlie.

The longdog powers in to attempt a pick-up.

As a result of the decline in foxhunting in many parts of the country which to be fair has not only been brought about by the antics of those opposed to it but also by the ceaseless urbanisation of the countryside, the population of foxes varies widely from location to location and with it, but on the whole, in inverse proportion so does the number of hares. Thus, on the marshes round where I live at present, hares are very few and far between, although they exist in very appreciable quantities not more than a few miles away, there being a stretch of tidal water in between.

Where there are fair numbers of hares, neither coursing nor beagling have much effect on them, not even to the point of controlling them, this being for the very good reason that both coursers and beaglers have one thing in common and this is an earnest desire to see large, healthy hare populations, doing all in their power to preserve the creatures. This can be quite vexatious in places where damage is being done to cropping, although this does not assume such serious proportions as it did in the days when large acreages of root crops were grown for animal feeding. The effect of an overlarge hare population on a field of swedes or turnips was one of the many burdens which a shepherd had to bear in the days of folded sheep.

Where hares have to be controlled in number, this is usually carried out by means of driving them to guns. It is an efficient means of reducing their ranks but, to mind, savours somewhat of the draconian. To my mind and I like to think to the minds of a good many other sportsmen, the hare exists for the longdog and the longdog for the hare.

One of the favourite ways of taking a hare in days gone by was by means of a gate net used in conjunction with the right sort of dog, usually a lurcher or a longdog, although I have come across collies which were by no means bad at the game. Unfortunately, this is a method which, except in a very few districts is no longer open to us, the main reason being that since so very few hedges are left in most parts of the country, the necessity for gates, let alone gate nets has ceased to exist. If, by any chance you are in a position to use such a net, then by all means try it out. You will need a dog which will quarter the field in much the same way as a gundog and it will have to be trained to herd its quarry towards you, as his owner. This is a fairly natural thing to do and most dogs will take to it, although this is one job where I think that I might prefer a lurcher to a longdog.

You will also need a gate net and this must be of adequate size, in other words a good bit larger than the gates that you use it on. Do not tie it to the gate; secure it to the top rail with some good sized stones with a few more to hold the bottom of it steady. It can then be relied upon to collapse upon the hare, thus enmeshing it. This way of securing the net was also a favourite with poachers, who, should they wish to depart in a hurry, saw no point in leaving their tackle behind them.

Two dogs turning their hare.

The main way in which hares are taken by longdogs these days is by straightforward coursing. For this two dogs are best so as to turn the hare and it will then be a fairly sure kill if the dogs have learned to run cunning. By this I mean for one of them to lie back and take the hare on its turn. The best way to get a dog into the way of doing this is to run it at rabbits a good deal. These will give it the idea quicker than any other means and is one of the reasons why serious coursing men refuse to slip their dogs on to the lesser game when exercising them, very little in the way of coursing points being awarded for a kill.

There is also a certain amount of so called best of three coursing these days. This consists of running a single dog at a hare, having given it sufficient law and is decided not on points but on straightforward kills. For this game a dog with a good deal of stamina is required and this is where the deerhound and saluki blooded longdogs come into their own. If you decide to take up this form of recreation, bear in mind that you will be expected to wager quite large sums of money and that settling day is frequently not without its problems, depending naturally on what sort of company you keep and how good you happen to be at the rough stuff.

Conclusions

So what does it come down to in the end? If you have reached this stage in the book, whether you agree with all that I have to say or not, you will probably have reached some conclusions of your own. Get around a bit amongst those who run longdogs and see if your ideas are reinforced or otherwise. I formed fairly definite opinions on the different sorts of running dogs ages ago but not such definite ones that they have not bent as the years have rolled by. I suppose that just as my horizons and outlook has altered, so to some extent have the characteristics of the dogs I have owned. Dogs which are the tops in the African bush assume somewhat different proportions when used in the conditions pertaining in the Home Counties and, amongst other conclusions I have reached, one is that I must have hunted with my last Irish wolfhound.

In my view it comes down to two sorts of longdog in the end, possibly three types if one includes salukis and their outcrosses. On the face of it the saluki seems to be just about the ideal hunting dog being just about the right size for an all rounder, fast enough to take any sort of game that it may be faced with, with plenty of stamina and of sound conformity. No doubt, if you get a good one, it has to be something exceptional but so much rests in the luck of the draw. I think it is no coincidence that the majority of men who like to gamble on the outcome of the 'best of three' type of course favour salukis. The greyhound/deerhound hybrid, a cross I have been using and breeding for some time now, are, in my view hard to fault for they have everything that I look for in a sporting dog. But I do think it is important that the sire is a sensible greyhound and the dam of coursing deerhound stock. At present I am seriously considering the introduction of whippet blood into the mix. The more I see of these little dogs, the better I come to like them.

As an all rounder the whippet is difficult to find fault with, the only snag being that they are a bit on the small side for hare and fox, although when you find the right sort of whippet, the terrier blood seems to become very evident when engaging Charlie. The other great thing about them, of course, is that, should you fancy showing your dog as well as working it, a whippet is one with which you could get as far as Cruft's. It beats me why anyone should want to keep a lurcher or a crossbred longdog solely for the purpose of exhibiting it at lurcher shows, and yet there are a growing number of those who do. If they are so keen on the showing game to the exclusion of all else, then why not go in for pure bred whippets, salukis or deerhounds and be done with it?

Index